Grab 'n Stab

The man rushed Slocum, his butcher knife thrusting straight for the gut. Slocum twisted away at the last possible instant, grabbed the brawny wrist, more to get his own balance than to prevent a second slash, and then used his own blade where it would do the most good. His cut was aimed at the man's throat. He got him across the eyes.

"Ya blinded me!" The man lashed out with his knife, flailing wildly. Blood gushed from the wound into the man's eyes. Slocum might have stepped away and left his foe thrashing about.

Instead, he judged his distance, and when the opportunity came, he took it. His knife sank up to the hilt in the man's chest, puncturing his heart. The Butcher died way too easily.

Slocum stepped away, panting harshly. He wiped his blade off on the man's leather apron, then went to get his horse.

"Lookin' fer this?" Another of the Butchers held the reins of Slocum's gelding in one hand. In the other he held a six-shooter. "Saw what you done to me friend. Now it's time fer ya to suffer a mite 'fore I slice you up . . ."

DON'T MISS THESE
ALL-ACTION WESTERN SERIES
FROM THE BERKLEY PUBLISHING GROUP

THE GUNSMITH by J. R. Roberts

Clint Adams was a legend among lawmen, outlaws, and ladies. They called him . . . the Gunsmith.

LONGARM by Tabor Evans

The popular long-running series about Deputy U.S. Marshal Custis Long—his life, his loves, his fight for justice.

SLOCUM by Jake Logan

Today's longest-running action Western. John Slocum rides a deadly trail of hot blood and cold steel.

BUSHWHACKERS by B. J. Lanagan

An action-packed series by the creators of Longarm! The rousing adventures of the most brutal gang of cutthroats ever assembled—Quantrill's Raiders.

DIAMONDBACK by Guy Brewer

Dex Yancey is Diamondback, a Southern gentleman turned con man when his brother cheats him out of the family fortune. Ladies love him. Gamblers hate him. But nobody pulls one over on Dex . . .

WILDGUN by Jack Hanson

The blazing adventures of mountain man Will Barlow—from the creators of Longarm!

TEXAS TRACKER by Tom Calhoun

J. T. Law: the most relentless—and dangerous—manhunter in all Texas. Where sheriffs and posses fail, he's the best man to bring in the most vicious outlaws—for a price.

JAKE LOGAN

SLOCUM AND THE SCHUYLKILL BUTCHERS

JOVE BOOKS, NEW YORK

THE BERKLEY PUBLISHING GROUP
Published by the Penguin Group
Penguin Group (USA) Inc.
375 Hudson Street, New York, New York 10014, USA
Penguin Group (Canada), 90 Eglinton Avenue East, Suite 700, Toronto, Ontario M4P 2Y3, Canada
(a division of Pearson Penguin Canada Inc.)
Penguin Books Ltd., 80 Strand, London WC2R 0RL, England
Penguin Group Ireland, 25 St. Stephen's Green, Dublin 2, Ireland (a division of Penguin Books Ltd.)
Penguin Group (Australia), 250 Camberwell Road, Camberwell, Victoria 3124, Australia
(a division of Pearson Australia Group Pty. Ltd.)
Penguin Books India Pvt. Ltd., 11 Community Centre, Panchsheel Park, New Delhi—110 017, India
Penguin Group (NZ), 67 Apollo Drive, Rosedale, North Shore 0632, New Zealand
(a division of Pearson New Zealand Ltd.)
Penguin Books (South Africa) (Pty.) Ltd., 24 Sturdee Avenue, Rosebank, Johannesburg 2196,
South Africa

Penguin Books Ltd., Registered Offices: 80 Strand, London WC2R 0RL, England

SLOCUM AND THE SCHUYLKILL BUTCHERS

A Jove Book / published by arrangement with the author

PRINTING HISTORY
Jove edition / August 2008

Cover illustration by Sergio Giovine.

For information, address: The Berkley Publishing Group,
a division of Penguin Group (USA) Inc.,
375 Hudson Street, New York, New York 10014.

ISBN: 978-0-515-14510-6

JOVE®
Jove Books are published by The Berkley Publishing Group,
a division of Penguin Group (USA) Inc.
375 Hudson Street, New York, New York 10014.
JOVE is a registered trademark of Penguin Group (USA) Inc.
The "J" design is a trademark belonging to Penguin Group (USA) Inc.

PRINTED IN THE UNITED STATES OF AMERICA

10 9 8 7 6 5 4 3 2 1

1

The morning sun felt good on John Slocum's face as he rode slowly across the Montana grasslands. There had been too much trouble behind him back in Idaho to remain there even one day longer. A change of scenery was definitely needed, and South Dakota struck him as a good place to head, especially if he had to cross terrain as lovely as Montana to get there.

He pulled back on the gelding's reins and wiped his face with his bandanna. The day had yet to warm up, but he had been feeling poorly for the past week. Bad water might be the cause, or an insect bite he had gotten on his neck a while ago that had never quite healed. Slocum was not sure as to the cause of his discomfort, but all he really knew was that the three brothers he had tangled with back in Idaho over a poker game were a quicker way to die than a bellyache from polluted water or fever from a mosquito bite. Slocum laughed without a trace of humor. Dying of cholera was preferable to dealing with the Driggs boys and their notion of what made for a fair game of chance. He had won and that had violated their single rule: One of the Driggs brothers won. Always. They might have the entire town of Stanley convinced that this was the only way to play draw poker, but Slocum preferred to follow more conventional rules. A pair of aces beat a pair of deuces. Always.

He shivered uncontrollably and looked ahead at the distant purple-cloaked mountains, wondering if he could find shelter there before the spring thunderstorm coming at him from the north struck. Dying of ague was nothing he fancied. But he knew he was not going to die of cholera. He might be a little woozy and have a low-grade fever, but he wasn't going to die of anything as terrible as that. He still had places to go and things to do. All Slocum had to do was figure out where they were and what they were.

Pulling down his hat shielded his eyes from the sun. He found a faint trail leading eastward toward the mountains. From long experience, he knew the rocky slopes looked close but might be more than a day's ride off. That didn't matter to him. It didn't matter if he was a few days late getting to wherever he was going. Not being trapped out in the open mattered more at the moment.

"Giddyap," he told his gelding, putting his spurs to strong flanks. The horse neighed and trotted off. Slocum guessed the horse was equally unwilling to get soaked by a rain shower, and it was not even suffering from a fever. Riding along at a decent clip, Slocum let his mind wander. His memories skipped over the Driggs boys and lingered on Madeleine LeSur, a dance hall girl in Stanley. He knew that was not her name and that she had never been within a thousand miles of France in spite of her elaborate stories and Continental airs. More likely, she hailed from somewhere south of Montana. Perhaps Texas, since there had been a hint of drawl to her speech that she could not hide.

He had spent some glorious nights with her before they had grown tired of each other. She was yet another reason he had decided it was high time to move on.

Slocum rocked in the saddle when his horse came to a sudden halt as it topped a rise in the barely visible road.

"What's wrong?" Slocum's hand strayed for the Colt

Navy slung in his cross-draw holster. His horse had shied at more rattlers in the past few hours than he could remember. A quick look around the trail and rocks nearby showed nothing slithering or hissing. But ahead in a grassy meadow, he spotted what must have brought his horse up short. The distance was too great to make out the details, but at least a hundred head of cattle were being driven northward. He pulled down the brim of his hat against the morning sun and counted eight drovers.

"That what you wanted me to look at? Greenhorns trying to move cattle?" Slocum snorted. The cowboys had no clue how to keep the beeves moving in the desired direction. Twice as he watched, the herd edged either east or west and almost got away from the men. The riders consistently clustered in the wrong spots, allowing the cattle to follow their own lead more than once. Slocum let out a whoop of amusement when the cattle reached an arroyo and doubled back. The best the cowboys could do was trot alongside on the banks of the deep, sandy cut and wait for the cattle to tire themselves out.

"Think I could get a job as range boss?" Slocum had been a drover more times than he could remember, and trail boss a few times. The last trip from Texas to an Abilene, Kansas, railhead had been the straw that broke the camel's back. Rustlers had reduced the size of the herd, and when he reached Kansas, the authorities had claimed the cows were infected with Texas fever. It had taken more than arguing to get the papers signed and the cattle on trains bound for Chicago. Slocum had bribed the sheriff, the mayor, and the judge. The slim profit he had made for his troubles had won him a tirade from the herd's owner when he got back to Texas.

The inept riders finally raced down into the arroyo ahead of the cattle, and caused them to mill about before turning around and heading back northward. This time the cattle were held to their course by the very ravine that had permitted their brief escape.

"Boys, you're gonna run off any meat those beeves might have on them if you don't work harder," Slocum said. He watched the eight drovers get their herd out of the arroyo and back into the meadow, heading straight into the teeth of the storm surging down from Canada. Slocum shook his head. He wanted no part of keeping those cows from stampeding once they were pelted with rain and hail and faced with lightning and thunder.

Shivering as he rode, Slocum knew he would never make it to the mountains and the dubious shelter of a cave. Turning from the trail, he angled southward toward a grove of white-barked trees that offered some small shelter against the building storm. Slocum reached the overhanging limbs of the beech trees just as the first raindrops began splatting wetly all around him. Although he knew it was dangerous camping near a tree in a lightning storm, he didn't much care. His fever had peaked, and maybe getting struck by a solid bolt of lightning would cure what ailed him.

Slocum dismounted, then led his horse deeper into the woods until he found a spot where the horse would be sheltered from the worst of the wind and rain. Only then did he take his slicker and pull it around him. He knew keeping a fire burning would be a chore he wasn't up to. He rested with his back against a broad trunk and drew up his knees to pillow his head. Within minutes, in spite of the ominous crackle of thunder above and the steady swatting of rain against his oilskin slicker, he fell asleep.

Sometime during the night he came awake, not sure what brought him out of his stupor. He rubbed his eyes. The rain had subsided, leaving the ground wet and cool and fresh. The utter darkness of the forest prevented him from seeing anything—but he heard the soft squishing of footsteps coming closer. Slocum shrugged back his slicker and drew his six-shooter. If he had not drawn, he would have been dead.

His finger squeezed back as he sighted in on the foot-long tongue of orange flame leaping from the muzzle of a rifle. His attacker missed. Slocum did not.

"Jed, Jed," came the weak cry, and then nothing.

"He done shot Jed! Get him!"

Slocum rolled away as one bullet after another ripped into the tree trunk he had rested against. Splinters flew and sap covered him, but he kept moving. From the sounds in the forest, he faced no fewer than three others.

"You sure it's him?" came an aggrieved voice.

"Who else'd cut down Jed like that but a lawman?"

Slocum turned slowly, getting a better idea where his ambushers were in the forest. The one protesting was directly ahead. Slocum got off a shot that produced a loud yelp of pain. His shot had winged the man, not killed him. Slocum wasted no time regretting it. Rolling away, he easily avoided three more slugs seeking out his flesh.

He came to rest a few yards away, flat on his belly. The impenetrable darkness worked against him—and his attackers. They were no better able to see him than he could see them. He waited until he heard movement. He fired three times, once where he thought the man was, then a shot to either side. One of the three slugs found a target. He heard a grunt, followed by a falling body.

"We gotta get outta here," cried another. Slocum cursed his bad luck. He had misjudged how many were after him. There might be two more, and his spare ammo was in his saddlebags.

"He's out of bullets," said one. Slocum damned the man for either counting or guessing right that he rode with his hammer resting on an empty chamber.

"Don't care."

"He'll fetch a posse now that he knows where we are."

"Like hell he will. He can't raise no posse. If he could, he woulda brung 'em with him.

Slocum slid his six-gun into his holster and reached down to his boot top. His fingers closed around the hilt of a thick-bladed knife. Again, the darkness was his ally. He got to his feet and slipped out of his slicker, wadded it up, and heaved it as hard he could.

"There! There he is!"

He heard bullets ripping through his oilskin, but Slocum knew it was a small price to pay to locate the nearest of the gunmen. Moving like the wind, he slipped between the trees, found his target, and got behind him. Slocum grabbed a handful of long, greasy hair, yanked the head back, and slit the man's throat before he could cry out.

Easing the corpse to the ground, Slocum grabbed the man's six-shooter. He had no idea how many rounds were already spent, but even one more shot would work for him.

"Cormac, you all right?"

Only Slocum knew Cormac would have to speak out of a second mouth—one grinning from ear to ear across his throat—if he responded. The steady drip of blood onto the wet leaves soon stopped. Cormac was dead.

Slocum twisted about, found some thornbushes, and crouched down, waiting. During the war, he had been a sniper and had learned to be patient. If it took all day of waiting in the sun, perched on an uncomfortable tree branch waiting for a Yankee officer to show himself, so be it. A good shot would remove the enemy's leader and cause more confusion than a full-frontal cavalry assault.

He waited for what must have been five minutes. Doggedness paid off. He saw a tree limb swing back and forth as someone pushed it out of the way. Slocum fired directly under the branch, and was rewarded with a gasp of pain.

A second shot failed. Either he had picked up a six-shooter with only one round left, or the rain caused the ammo to misfire. He tried a third shot. Nothing. He tossed the pistol as hard as he could, and began sneaking through the forest in the direction of his horse. He had been lucky so far. Against so many men, his luck would run out eventually.

He slid down the slippery slope to the draw where he had

left his horse. The gelding whinnied and pawed at the ground. Slocum dropped to his belly and slid forward like a snake. He was glad he had been cautious when he saw the faint outline of a sentry nervously fingering a rifle. The man's silhouette against the clearing night sky provided enough target for Slocum.

He gathered his feet under him and launched. His toes slid against wet leaves as he lunged forward, his knife blade slashing viciously. He caught the man's arm and sent blood fountaining into the forest. But he had missed a clean kill.

The sentry dropped his rifle and ran for dear life. Slocum regained his balance, went to his horse, saddled up, and rode directly southward. He had no idea what direction the ambushers had come from, but going any other direction would take him deeper into the forest. He wanted open space around him to ride hard and fast. Taking on an unknown number of backshooters wasn't something he wanted to deal with at the moment.

Staying low, keeping the horse walking at a steady clip, Slocum left the murderous owlhoots far behind. His hands shook, and he felt weaker than a newborn kitten, but he was alive. That was more than a couple of the men back in the forest could claim.

He patted his gelding's neck, then dismounted after riding what he estimated to be a couple miles. Slocum fumbled about in his saddlebags, found his spare ammo, and reloaded. Only then did he take the time to swallow a long drink of water from his canteen. His fever had broken during the night, but had left him weak and thirsty.

"Dangerous country, Montana," he told his horse. "Better not stand around too long. They might have been road agents looking for an easy robbery, but they didn't run when I plugged a pair of them. Even said they thought I might be the law."

At that notion, Slocum laughed harshly. He kept his distance from the law whenever possible. After the war, he had returned to the family farm in Georgia. His brother

Robert had been killed during Pickett's Charge, and their ma and pa were long dead. He had begun farming, doing a little hunting on property that had been in the Slocum family since the days of George I, only to have a carpetbagger judge take a fancy to the land. The judge wanted it for a stud farm and had conjured up nonexistent taxes that had never been paid. When he and a hired gunman had ridden out to seize the property, they had gotten more than they expected.

Slocum had buried both of them by the springhouse, gotten on his horse, and ridden west, never looking back. All the way across the Mississippi, wanted posters for killing a federal judge had dogged his heels. Even when he reached the Rockies, the reward on his head lured bounty hunters and got marshals excited about the prospect of arresting him.

The men in the forest were dead wrong about him being a lawman. Slocum smiled wryly. Some of them were more than dead wrong—they were dead. That the men with them had not run worried him. They had something more in mind than robbery or catching themselves a sheriff by surprise.

More reason to get through the badlands and deeper into South Dakota. He kept riding south until sunrise, then stopped when he saw a small stream promising water and a cooling bath.

He let his horse drink its fill as he sat on the streambed and washed out his bandanna, then wrapped the soaked cloth around his neck.

Slocum had reached out to cup water in his palm and take a drink when he saw a man reflected in the turbulent water. He jerked to one side as he reached for his six-shooter. A rifle butt slammed into the side of his head, and the rising sun suddenly disappeared and darkness closed in all around him.

When he came to, every bone in his body ached. He tried to turn, and found himself slung over the back of his horse. His feet and hands had been tied together under the gelding's belly, and he had been lashed into place with a few quick turns of rope around his waist and the saddle horn. Every step was pure agony, but Slocum did not cry out. If he could overhear what was being said around him, he might have a better chance at escape.

A quiet murmur rose.

"That one of 'em, Marshal?" someone nearby called out. He heard others shouting the same question.

"Why else would I be bringin' the varmint to town?"

Slocum let the motion of the horse flop his head about so he could get a better look at the man riding beside him. All he saw was a curly mop of sandy hair poking out from under the brim of a battered black hat—and the glint of sunlight off a badge.

Twisting his wrists about only chafed his skin. Slocum tried to slip free of the ropes binding his hands so securely. His ankles would still be tied together, but he would stand a better chance of getting away if he could grab for a six-shooter.

"Don't go hurtin' yerse'f none, mister," said the marshal. "I know you're awake. I saw the instant you came to. Thought your head might be so hard I couldn't conk you unconscious fer more'n an hour or two, and I was right."

Slocum did not reply. His belly was on fire, and breathing was such a chore he might as well have been under water. When they stopped, Slocum got a glimpse of a jailhouse. "Sharpesville Town Jail" was lettered above the door.

"Where's Sharpesville?" he grated out. Then he was pulled off the horse and thrown to the ground. All Slocum could do was lie on his back and stare into the brilliant blue sky dotted with a few puffy white clouds. It would have been a beautiful day except he was in the custody of a town marshal.

"Right under yer feet, that's where." The marshal laughed harshly. "Let me change that. It's the dirt under yer worthless ass." He reached down and grabbed the ropes binding Slocum's wrists and dragged his prisoner into the jail.

"Luther, git yer carcass out here. We got ourse'ves a visitor."

"He one of 'em, Marshal?" came the squeaky voice from the back of the calaboose.

"Who else'd I bring in, you fool?"

Luther came from the back. He was hardly sixteen, from the look of it. When he spoke again, there was no break in his voice. He rumbled with a deeper bass, but before he got to the end of his sentence, his voice cracked again.

"What do you want me to do with him, Marshal?"

"Throw the son of a bitch into a cell and then lock the door, that's what. You taitched in the head, Luther? He's a *prisoner*. What else would we do with 'im?"

"Nothing, I suppose, Marshal," the youngster said, looking embarrassed and not a little angry at being ragged on like that for no good reason.

Slocum tried to stand, but his legs refused to hold him. Luther put a supporting arm around Slocum's shoulders and guided him in to the rear of the jail. Slocum fell facedown when the marshal planted a foot smack on his behind and shoved.

"Don't go coddlin' the son of a bitch none, Luther. He's a killer through and through."

"Yes, sir, I can see that," Luther said uncertainly.

He opened a cell door and shoved Slocum inside. Luther's heart wasn't in it. He didn't have the gusto the marshal showed with his butt-kicking.

Slocum flopped around and looked up as Luther closed the door and hastily locked it. The cell was going to be hard to escape, Slocum saw right away. It was made from two-inch-wide iron straps riveted together. He guessed it went under the floor and up into the ceiling, as well as into the stone wall behind him. The only sure way out was through the door Luther had just secured.

The young man looked at him uneasily, refusing to meet

his gaze, then ran from the cell. He did not bother pulling shut the door leading into the marshal's office.

"What we gonna do with him, Marshal?"

The answer brought back chills to Slocum's spine that had nothing to do with a fever.

"Why, Luther, old son, we're gonna hang 'im as soon as we kin throw together some gallows."

2

The thick-barred door rattled when he shook it hard. Some jail cells looked ferociously hard to escape, but the locks gave easily. The marshal had put the best lock he could find on the iron under Slocum's fingers. Slocum kicked at the door, hoping to jolt it open.

"You make any more noise in there, I'll come back and whup you good," the marshal of Sharpesville bellowed from the office. He got up from his desk, peered through the doorway at Slocum, then slammed the wood door hard, leaving Slocum alone in the tiny cell block.

Slocum was more circumspect with his attempts to free himself after that. While his noise had forced the marshal to close the outer door, he did not doubt the lawman would beat him within an inch of his life if he made more noise. Then the hangman's noose would drop over his throat. Just thinking about that made Slocum reach up and run his calloused fingers over his throat. Sweat stained his collar and turned his fingers damp.

He spun about and began to survey the cell more carefully. The two-inch-wide straps vanished into the floor. He dropped to his knees and began digging until he got down far enough to realize he was entirely enclosed in the cage.

To make certain, he drew the edge of his belt buckle along the wall, worrying at the crumbling mortar. He got several inches free only to find what he had feared. The iron straps had been mortared over, the middle of a sandwich formed by the outer wall and the inner concrete.

Snorting in disgust, he wiped his hands on his jeans and then dropped onto the cot. The thin pallet was almost worse than no mattress at all, but Slocum stretched out and stared at the ceiling. The crisscross of the iron straps taunted him. Restless, he got to his feet and began pacing.

He couldn't get out, and he couldn't make head or tail of why he had been brought in the way he had. In spite of the wanted posters scattered throughout the West, he doubted the marshal had recognized him as a judge killer and had brought him in. It seemed like something else had put the bug up the lawman's ass. Slocum gave the door one last rattle to convince himself he was not going to get out this easily.

Craning his neck around, he saw a sliver of light under the door leading into the office. When a shadow passed across the light, he caught his breath. The marshal might have left. He looked up, then climbed like a circus monkey until he dangled from the overhead straps.

"Luther, Luther, come quick!" Slocum waited for the youth to come rushing in.

Luther did, but not with wide-eyed astonishment at the fact that the cell seemed to be empty. The young man took a step in to the cell block, looked around, and then slowly lifted his eyes until they were fixed on Slocum.

"You kin hurt yerself hangin' like a spider," he said.

Slocum dropped to the floor, brushed off his hands, and stared at the reluctant deputy.

"I seen men do that before," Luther said. "'Sides, the marshal tole me to be on the lookout fer tricks."

"Why'd he throw me in here? I just rode into the territory on my way east. I haven't had time to do anything illegal."

"Now, you know why you're in there, mister."

"Tell me. Pretend I'm a bit daft." Slocum waited for Luther to take a couple steps closer. Men did that when they talked. Luther kept his distance.

"Men tried that, too. Some real desperadoes."

"I don't look desperate?" Slocum almost laughed at this.

"You got the look of a hired gun, that's what you look like," Luther said.

This caused Slocum to sober. "I'm no gunfighter. All I am is a cowboy riding to South Dakota."

"There's no reason fer me to keep talkin' to you," Luther said, stepping away. Not once had he come close enough for Slocum to make a grab. Even if he had pulled the young man into the bars, what then? Luther had left the keys in the outer office. He might kill the boy out of spite, but that wouldn't get him out of this iron cage.

More than that, he had no call to hurt the young man. It wasn't Luther's fault the marshal had taken to throwing anyone riding through his territory into a cell, then promising to hang them.

"Why's he want to stretch my neck?"

"You sound almost as if you don't know," Luther said. "He tole you to keep silent. You do that. I'll fetch some food in a couple hours. Don't go thinkin' on jumpin' me then neither. All I have to do is set the food on the floor, then push it to you with a stick." To illustrate his point, Luther reached behind him and brandished a long wooden rod that had been leaning against the wall. He used it like a schoolmarm might stab at a blackboard with a pointer.

Slocum saw the slot cut at ankle level in the cell door. All Luther said was true. A tray with food could be shoved into the cell. The best Slocum could hope for was stealing a knife or fork to use as a weapon or a tool to pry open the lock.

"You don't," Luther said out of the clear blue.

"I don't what?" Slocum looked up, startled. He had been making his plans once he got fed.

"You don't git no silverware. You eat with yer fingers or you don't eat at all. I tole you, mister, they's tried 'bout ever' trick in the book." With that, Luther closed the door with a solid thunk.

Slocum held back a surge of burning fury. Getting angry would not free him from this hick town jail. Two more circuits of the cell convinced him that the only way he was likely to get out was to go to his death on a gallows.

Standing on tiptoe, Slocum peered out the tiny window set high in the outside wall. As if it weren't enough that the iron straps kept him fully imprisoned, the bars were firmly set in the window giving double barriers to his escape. He finally stepped back. The old jail must have been renovated by adding the iron cages. The marshal had not bothered changing any of the original cells, just added more reinforcement.

The next ten minutes were spent cursing the marshal for being such a belt-and-suspenders kind of lawman. Then Slocum began working on the lower door hinge using his belt buckle. The hinge pins were protected well, but were the weakest part of a secure cell.

They just weren't weak enough. Slocum was not the kind of man who gave up, but he had to take a break when his hands began cramping from holding the belt bucklc so tightly for so long. He rocked back on his heels and looked at his handiwork.

He laughed ruefully. "At this rate," he said to himself, "I'll be out in fifty years."

The matter was not quite that bad, but he had to make more progress if he wanted to escape before the end of the week. Only a portion of the hinge had been cut through. The entire pin had to be lifted from the hinges to swing the cell door outward enough to squeeze through. Then the real escape would start. He had to reach the outer office and deal with the marshal.

Slocum jumped when he heard the door into the office creaking open. He turned and flopped onto the cot so hard it almost gave way under him.

"You jist stay right where you are, mister," Luther said,

inching forward cautiously. He pushed a tray with food ahead of him, using the toe of his boot to move it. When he lined up the tray and the slot in the bottom of the cell door, he used his long stick to poke it into the cell, as he had promised.

"How long do I have to finish?" Slocum asked. His mind still worked on ways to escape.

"As long as it takes. I kin wait you out."

"What should I do with the tray and plate when I'm done?" Slocum eyed the plate of beans with no real hunger gnawing at his belly. A hunk of dry bread was all he got in the way of an eating utensil.

"Leave it or shove it back outside. Don't make no nevermind to me."

"Why?" Slocum looked up sharply.

"This here's yer last meal, that's why. They's hangin' you at sunrise. Didn't see no reason to waste a good breakfast on you."

Slocum looked over his shoulder, out the window into the chilly Montana night. He probably didn't have eight hours left before the necktie party began, with him as the honored guest.

Before he could say another word, Luther ducked back into the outer office. Slocum got a quick glimpse of the room. Luther was alone. If Slocum was going to get free, it had to be done right now.

Slocum grabbed the plate of beans and dumped the contents onto the tray. He grabbed the plate, moved so he got it through the iron straps, and judged distances. He might throw it at Luther when the youth came back in. Anger him, get him to rush forward, grab him. After that Slocum would have to play it by ear. Maybe the marshal would return and find Slocum with a stranglehold on his young deputy.

What if he didn't return until sunrise? Slocum would have to hold Luther for a powerful long time.

He gripped the plate, licked his lips, and was starting to

call out when the door opened a fraction of an inch. His luck was changing. He didn't even have to lure Luther back in to the cell block. Drawing back, Slocum waited to fling the plate.

"Don't," came a soft voice.

Slocum squinted to see a shapely shadow push the door open. For a brief instant, the woman was silhouetted by the coal-oil lamp burning on the marshal's desk. Then she was plunged into darkness as she pulled the squeaky door closed behind her.

It took him a few seconds to decide not to fling the plate at her, although she would make a better hostage than Luther. Whoever she was.

Slocum dropped the plate when he heard the rattle of keys. She stepped closer and held up the ring so she could better see the keys on it. She rapidly studied and discarded one after another until she selected one.

As she worked to wiggle the key into the door lock and free him, Slocum got a better look at her.

"You're about the prettiest deputy I ever did see," he said.

"I'm not a deputy." Her tone told him she was not in the mood for joshing. "There."

She yanked the door open and stepped away. He got a better look at her now and appreciated what he saw. Auburn hair fell to her shoulders and framed an oval face that might have been chiseled out of fine white china. Never had he seen a complexion so lovely. Or was it only the poor light in the jail? He stepped closer and got a better look at his savior. She was even prettier up close than from across the jail cell.

"Who are you?" he asked. The question took her aback.

"I expected you to ask why I was letting you out," she said.

"The reasons don't matter much. I want to know who to thank," Slocum said.

"Now aren't you the charmer?"

"Don't you mean full of blarney?" he said, again catching her off guard. "That's an Irish accent you've got, isn't it?"

"Don't waste time," she said pointedly. "I don't know when the marshal will get back."

"What happened to Luther?"

"You're worried I did something terrible to him?"

"He's mighty young to die," Slocum said.

She snorted contemptuously and shook her head. "In this sorry world, you can die at any instant."

"That'd be a real pity in your case," Slocum said. "Such a beautiful—"

"Enough of that guff, hear? I was not kidding when I said the marshal would be back soon. That doesn't give you much of a head start."

She spun to go. He grabbed her arm, but she pulled free and dashed from the cell. Slocum followed, stopping when he got to the door leading into the office. His benefactor had already left the jail. He looked around and saw his cross-draw holster with the Colt Navy in it hanging from a peg on the wall. Knowing he needed firepower as much as anything else, he strapped on his six-shooter and then grabbed a rifle from the rack.

As he did, a low moan sounded behind him. Slocum swung about, rifle cocked and leveled. Luther lay on the floor, curled up into a ball. From the bloody spot on the back of his skull, it was clear he had been slugged.

Slocum wasted no time. The boy was alive, and he was free. Or as free as he could be while still in Sharpesville. As he stepped into the cold night air, he saw light from a distant saloon glint off a badge.

Slocum lifted his rifle and fired at the marshal. He missed a clean shot, but heard the bullet rip through cloth and flesh. The distinctive sound was followed an instant later by a string of curses.

Not wasting an instant, Slocum got around the jailhouse and found his gelding tethered out back. The marshal had not bothered to remove the saddle. While Slocum would usually be angry at such lack of concern for a decent horse, now he was glad. He vaulted into the saddle and rode like the demons of hell were on his heels.

It turned out that they were. Fast. The marshal wasted no time browbeating half a dozen men into forming a posse.

Slocum rode in the dark, not knowing what direction he rode and fearing that a full, all-out gallop would put his horse in danger. The night was so inky black there was hardly light enough to see the road, much less any prairie-dog hole. For all he knew, he was retracing the route he had just covered and was riding back into the waiting arms of the Driggs boys.

Somehow, as smelly and ornery as they were, they were preferable company when his only other choice was a hangman.

The road twisted and turned and soon went into the mountains. He either rode north or south, since he had not encountered terrain like this riding from the west. He hoped he was headed south toward Wyoming. More than one summer had been passed there pleasantly enough, and Slocum knew the land just to the east of the Tetons like the back of his hand. The marshal of a jerkwater town like Sharpesville would not pursue him that far—his posse wouldn't let him. But if bounty hunters came after him, put on his trail by the marshal, he could lose them easily in familiar territory.

First, he had to reach it.

He kept looking at the night sky hoping to catch a glimpse of a familiar constellation. Heavy clouds masked the sky too much of the time for him to get a decent idea what direction he rode in. In his gut, Slocum felt that he was heading north and away from the possible haven of Wyoming.

Slowing when his horse began to tire, Slocum guided the gelding off the road and down into a rocky draw. Trees grew in profusion on both sides of the dried-up streambed, giving him added cover. He gave the horse its head to see where it might take him. Like an arrow, the horse found a shallow pool of water and began drinking noisily. Slocum dropped to the ground and washed his face. Only then did he pull the horse back.

A faint sound came to him that chilled his soul.

The steady clop-clop of horses' hooves told him the marshal had wasted no time tracking him. Someone in the posse must be a damned fine scout to see any spoor on such a dark night. Then the answer came when Slocum spotted a sudden flash of light. The marshal had brought lanterns.

He swore under his breath, grabbed his horse's reins, and led it up the far side of the ravine. He wanted to lose himself in the lightly wooded area, circle around when he could, and ride as hard as he could for someplace that wasn't Montana.

Knowing how easy it was to get turned around in dark woods, Slocum proceeded cautiously, judging each step so it took him slightly uphill. It would be his death if he inadvertently veered to his right, as men in forests and in desert country were likely to do, and circled back into the posse's guns.

A broad meadow beckoned. If Slocum could ride across to the far side, he was sure he could evade the hunters on his trail. The only problem he saw with that was a small campfire not twenty yards off. He would be noticed if he crossed the open space. The marshal would ask, and whoever camped in the meadow would put the posse onto Slocum in a flash.

Carefully making his way, he stayed just inside the forested area, out of sight, moving slowly. Too slowly. He heard thrashing and crashing in the woods he had just traversed. The marshal had caught up with him too fast. Slocum drew the rifle out and cocked it. The metallic click as it levered a round into the firing chamber sounded like a clap of thunder to him.

Just then the marshal and six mounted men burst from

the woods. Slocum caught his first bit of luck. They spotted the campfire and made for it like a vulture for dead meat.

What happened next caused Slocum to stand a little straighter and lift his rifle to his shoulder. The posse circled the campfire and whoever lay asleep pushed back a blanket and stood. Bright steel flashed in the dim light. Then all hell broke loose and fell on the marshal and his deputies.

From nowhere came a dozen men, all swinging wickedly long knives and what looked like meat cleavers. The marshal and two of his men got off a shot before they died. They were hacked and slashed and pulled from horseback. Once they were on the ground, their attackers savagely chopped at them repeatedly. Slocum found himself frozen to the spot, unable to move.

Again, luck rode with him. From behind him in the forest came a dozen more men. One passed within feet of him, grunting and huffing and puffing as he waddled along. The mountain of a man swung a huge meat cleaver as he passed, but what caught Slocum's attention most was the leather apron he wore. The man would have been more at home in a butcher shop with that bloodstained apron wrapped around him.

"Git 'em, boys!"

The cry caused a new flurry of viciousness. Slocum knew that nothing could have remained of the marshal and his posse by the time the butchers were finished. The sight of one man holding an arm aloft caused Slocum's belly to knot. These weren't ordinary killers.

Moving as quietly as possible, aware that the second wave of killers had come from the direction he turned, Slocum melted into the woods. It had been a hell of a night ranging from a lovely, mysterious woman freeing him from jail to a slaughter of monumental proportions in the Montana hills.

It was definitely time for him to hightail it.

3

Slocum got only as far as the road meandering through the forest before he heard even more outlaws coming in his direction. Tugging on his horse's reins, he guided the gelding to a spot where the horse found patches of tasty grass and began gently cropping at it. The bridle and bit got in the horse's way and frustrated it, but the promise of food was enough to keep the horse busy while Slocum clutched his rifle and waited.

A dozen more of the leather-apron–clad men wielding cleavers and long knives trooped along the road. Their leader stopped them and spoke rapidly. Slocum tried to make out the words, but couldn't. Whatever the man said split the group into three parts. Some continued along the road, another group stayed, and the rest followed their boss into the woods past where Slocum waited with his breath held so long that he thought his lungs would explode. Only when the last of the men trooped on to join the rest of their brutal band did Slocum let out the pent-up air. His lungs felt as if he had sucked in fire, and his heart hammered fast enough to make a vein pulse on his forehead.

He tried to make an estimate of how many leather-apron–clad men there were. He stopped counting at thirty.

A small army had invaded this part of Montana and made life even harder for him. Not only did he have to get away from men likely to kill him on sight, there would be a great suspicion back in Sharpesville that he had done in the marshal and his posse if he tried to report their deaths. Not dealing with the Driggs brothers looked more foolish to him by the instant.

Settling down on his haunches, Slocum waited. He couldn't run, and he couldn't fight. The only consolation was the heavy cloud layer cutting off all starlight. Holding his hand in front of his face, Slocum could hardly see it. The butchers roaming the woods were not likely to spot him either as long as his horse remained quiet.

Even as the thought ran through his head, the gelding reared. Slocum was quick to grab the reins and hold it down, patting it and whispering softly to soothe the frightened animal. Although anything might have spooked the horse, Slocum knew the real cause. The ground vibrated from marching feet as the horde returned from the campsite in the meadow. Slocum gritted his teeth as they came nearer. If they found him, he would go down fighting. Better to die that way than to be captured and then hacked up like a steer.

The men passed him again, not ten feet away, laughing and singing bawdy songs. Slocum tensed as he recognized what they sang. During the war, Federals from Pennsylvania had delighted in the same song. He had spied on their encampment just before the battle of Spotsylvania. Those soldiers had been Irish miners before joining the army. The song of dying in the mines and letting the ghosts roam free came easily to the lips of these men. As hard as it had been for Slocum to believe, fighting pitched battles had been safer for them than toiling in the coal mines.

They were a long way from home if they were Pennsylvania coal miners.

"Back home, boys," called a man brandishing what might have been a Yankee bayonet like it was a baton and he was the drum major leading a Fourth of July parade. The men fell in behind, forming two columns. As they began hiking away into the night, they broke into boisterous song again. If there had been any doubt in Slocum's mind where they were from, this erased it. Miners. Pennsylvania miners.

He puzzled over what they were doing in Montana—and why they wielded their deadly weapons with such ferocity. The marshal and his deputies had had no chance at all against the overwhelming force. Shrugging off this knob of curiosity poking into his brain, Slocum sidled back and started to mount. If he rode quietly enough, he could find the main road without being heard by the miners.

He swung into the saddle and walked his horse out, heading in the direction opposite that taken by the miners, only to find himself facing eight more. These men were mounted and herding a couple dozen head of cattle. He had come upon them so fast he didn't have time to go to ground again.

Brazening it out was his only hope. Slocum pulled his hat low to hide his face, stood in the stirrups, and bellowed, "Whatcha doin', takin' yer time like that? Git them cows movin'."

"Aw, you try keepin' 'em all together," complained the man riding in front of the beeves.

"You're on the wrong side. You drive 'em. They ain't sheep that'll follow you," Slocum said, trying to imitate an Irish accent. He did not think he did a very good job, but the drovers paid no heed and accepted him as one of their own.

"You show us, damn your eyes."

Slocum only grunted in response. The longer he talked and tried to match the miners' speech and inflection, the more likely he was to get caught. The memory of those bloody knives and cleavers sent a chill through him. He pulled to the left, away from the knot of riders, and circled the nervous herd. While stampeding them might give him a few seconds' head start, he had no idea if he would gallop into still more of the Pennsylvanians. The entire countryside was crawling with them, and he had no idea how many more he might find without wanting to.

Keeping his head down, he slid his lariat from the leather thong holding it to his saddle. Slocum swatted the rumps of a couple cows and got them moving, pushing the others ahead. He left it to the other riders to keep the sides of the herd from getting off the road. As he rode, Slocum waited for the chance to slip back and then vanish into the night. But the others were too intent on watching how he worked to allow that.

Slocum had never been accused of being too good for a job before. Whatever he did he did well and left it at that, but now he was the teacher and any of his willing students might realize he was not one of their gang. Worse than being stuck at the rear of the herd, the sun was rising. Dawn would eventually reveal him as an interloper.

Although the riders didn't wear the leather aprons or carry the sharp knives of their partners, all were armed and looked as if they were able to handle their six-shooters.

"We're almost there," called a rider to Slocum's left. "Keep them dogs movin'."

"Dogies," Slocum said reflexively.

"Whatever you want to call 'em, they're gonna be breakfast! Can't wait to bite into a good, fresh steak. 'Specially if it's been rustled!"

This set off a round of argument over what the best part of a cow was. Slocum let them argue and dropped back a ways. They noticed immediately. Two of the rustlers slowed to hang back with him.

As the cattle turned this way and that, Slocum caught sight of the brands. At least three different brands showed that the boast about dining on freshly stolen beef was true. Slocum wasn't above stealing a cow or two himself, and in his day had driven large herds of rustled cattle, but being caught with these few paltry head of rustled cattle would put him squarely in the camp with the leather-aproned killers.

Rustling was one thing. Ranchers didn't like losing their precious cattle and were inclined to shoot first. That risk came with the crime. But being implicated in the murder of seven men, the marshal and six deputies, made the rustling even riskier. Slocum quickly dismounted and waved at the two men heading his way.

"Horse got a rock under its shoe. Go on. I'll catch up."

"Don't know we kin herd like you. How'd a hard-rock miner like you ever learn? We kin wait. Might be better with the sun up so we kin see what we're doin'."

"You'll do fine," Slocum assured them. "Lookee there! One's gettin' away!" Slocum pointed to draw attention away from himself. The cattle had obeyed once they learned they couldn't fool him. It would take the herd a while before they realized the rustlers driving them were complete greenhorns.

"Don't see nuthin'."

"Aw, Sean, 'course it's tryin' to get away. You as blind as you are stupid?" complained his partner.

"Shit," grumbled Sean. The pair of them wheeled about to tend their herd.

Slocum let them get out of sight before mounting. Backtracking along the road would go quicker than getting this far since he didn't have to keep a small herd of contrary beeves moving. Barely had he ridden a quarter mile when he saw a large knot of riders trotting in. Cursing, he veered off the road and made for a rise. All he needed to do was get over it and let the riders pass.

As he topped the ridge, Slocum's heart sank.

He was riding directly into a large camp of men. A dozen campfires were being stoked to cooking heat for breakfast. The stolen cattle wouldn't be butchered for this meal, but dinner might prove especially tasty for the dozens of men slowly coming awake as the first light of dawn lit the horizon.

He glanced over his shoulder and saw the riders coming up the slope after him. Without any other choice, Slocum kept riding, heading straight for the encampment. During the war he had seen companies with fewer men than this. Guessing at the numbers was a fool's errand. He stopped when he got to a hundred. Any of them raising an alarm would guarantee him a speedy death.

As he rode downhill, he saw his chance and took it. A deep gully afforded him momentary cover from both the camp and the riders higher above him on the hill. He dug his heels into the gelding's flanks and flew like the wind, slowing only when the horse began to falter. The rocky gully was still cloaked in darkness. Risking a broken leg would spell the end for both horse and rider.

"Whoa, slow, there, good," Slocum said, pulling back until the horse walked along at a sedate pace. Ahead, he saw pines rising up and promising shelter. He guided his horse out of the ravine straight to the wooded area. Once among the sheltering trees, he dismounted and tethered his horse.

A quick scout showed him he was some distance west of the main camp. To ride out now that the sun poked a fiery eye above the horizon was suicidal. Slocum resigned himself to hiding out until night fell before returning to the road out of the meadowland. There might be any number of other ways to leave this grassy expanse, but riding blindly looking for them would only get him caught. Already, outriders had mounted and begun a patrol around the outskirts of the camp. Such vigilance promised Slocum only sudden death if he showed himself.

He fished out some old jerky from his saddlebags and gnawed on it, sampling a few sips of water from his canteen. It was a poor breakfast, but better than getting a few slugs pumped into his belly. Slocum turned up the canteen and drained the last of the water. Making a sour face, he got to his feet and went exploring for a stream. When he got free of the rustlers, he wanted to ride without having to slow down for matters such as food and water.

Slocum began a careful examination of the ground, checking the slope and following it downward until he came to a small brook. As he filled the canteen, gruff voices came from farther downstream. Slocum threw himself facedown and wiggled like a snake to get out of sight. Three rustlers tromped toward where he lay barely shielded by a jacaranda bush.

"We got 'nuff fer the rest o' our lives," one said.

"Never got that," argued the second man. He wiped grimy hands on his shirt rather than washing them in the stream. Slocum rolled onto his side and drew his six-gun, ready to take out all three if they spotted him.

"He's right, Cory. Never be 'nuff. That's why we came out here. This is where the opportunity is, not with them sons of bitches mine owners."

"I miss Pennsylvania," said the first man.

"Hell, boyo, the whole lot of us come out here. Yer with friends good and true."

"To do what? Steal cows? Who wants to do that? I'm a damned miner."

"Damned right you are. We all are. Even the ones of us what spent that year or two in Chicago hackin' up livestock."

"I miss bustin' heads. When them mine owners shut us out . . ."

The trio walked farther along the stream, their backs now to Slocum. This muffled their voices, but he had learned enough. He'd bet every last nickel in his pocket these were members of the Molly Maguires, a roughneck miners' union responsible for killing scores of mine owners, their guards, and innocent people caught in the cross fire. But now that he knew who they were, he still had no idea why they had come to Montana. If they had been run out of Pennsylvania, they'd had to go somewhere, but why here?

Slocum frowned as he remembered what one had said about their thieving. They were stealing anything not nailed down. And, Slocum suspected, even if it was nailed down, the Molly Maguires would steal the nails.

He didn't think the three miners would find his horse. As reckless as it was, Slocum headed down the stream to see where the men had come from. Hiding behind one thin-boled pine not a dozen feet from the camp allowed him to see what they had stacked in untidy piles. His mouth watered when he saw how much food they had piled up. If they weren't more careful, they would attract every hungry bear in Montana to this veritable feast.

Another pile caught his eye. He had seen enough of the rectangular cases in his day to know that they contained close to fifty carbines. The U.S. Army seal stenciled on the side told him how busy the miners had been. They had stolen an arms shipment. With the army so touchy about Indians making off with stolen firearms, half the soldiers in the territory must be hunting for the weapons. The miners either didn't realize that or didn't care.

From their huge numbers, Slocum thought they just didn't give a good goddamn.

He had started to walk over to another pile that might have been heavy canvas moneybags when he heard a twig crack behind him. Spinning, he drew his six-shooter and pointed it. His heart leaped into his throat. All three of the men had sneaked up on him and he had not heard—he had been too engrossed in figuring out what he could steal.

"Son of a bitch. Who're you?"

"The gent with a six-shooter pointed at your gut," Slocum said. He motioned with his Colt Navy where he wanted the trio to move.

They charged with bull-throated roars that drowned out the first two reports from his six-gun. The .37-caliber pistol wasn't heavy enough to stop the man nearest to him. For that, Slocum thought he would have needed a buffalo gun. Both of his slugs hit the man square in the center of the chest, but never slowed him.

With a deep growl, he threw his arms around Slocum

and squeezed. Slocum grunted as his arms were clamped to his sides. He pulled the trigger a third time. This got the miner's attention. Slocum staggered back when he was suddenly released from the crushing embrace.

"He shot off my balls!" The man grabbed his privates and bent over.

Slocum got his balance, judged distance, and launched a kick that drove the toe of his boot into the point of the man's chin.

He had removed one of the three. The other two were going for their guns. Slocum emptied his six-shooter into the one closest to getting his hogleg out and into action. One bullet took the man in the temple, ending his life instantly.

Slocum ducked under wild fire from the third man, dived, and rolled. He frantically grabbed for the second man's fallen pistol. Somehow, he came up with it. His accuracy was far better than the remaining gunman's. A hunk of hot lead ripped out the miner's throat.

Already, he heard an outcry from other miners only yards away. Slocum threw down the pistol he had taken and made tracks for the pine tree he had used to survey the stolen property. He stiffened and tried to fold himself entirely behind the tree trunk as the others rushed up. Slocum caught sight of bright sunlight glinting off meat cleavers and knives.

If he tried to stay hidden, he would be quickly found. Slocum forced himself to walk slowly away to not draw attention.

"Did them damned fools kill each other?" demanded a gruff voice.

Slocum got deeper into the woods, then broke out in a dead run. The time had passed for him to try to remain quiet. He thrashed about, then stopped and listened hard, hoping he would hear nothing behind. He took off at top speed again when he heard several of the miners coming after him. They were not trackers and blundered about, but there were enough of them to form a line and come through the woods, so someone would see him.

Gasping for air, Slocum found his horse. The gelding looked up at him, white rims around its brown eyes.

"I got to admit, I'm scared, too," Slocum said, swinging into the saddle. The horse reared when a bullet splatted into a tree trunk not three feet away. Slocum kept control and wheeled the horse about, staying low and urging as much speed as possible.

The branches cut and lashed at his head, but Slocum knew the penalty for slowing now. More slugs whined through the air. None came close, but the mere act of firing on him would alert others in the gang.

And there were a lot of them, from what Slocum had seen.

"This way! He went this way! A spy! Fifty dollars to the man who gits him!"

Slocum doubted the offer would be taken back if they happened to kill him. If anything, there might be a bonus in the reward for his dead carcass.

He hit the road at a full gallop. His horse was strong, but could only run this fast for a few miles.

Slocum hoped it would be enough.

4

He felt rather than heard the bullet. Slocum jerked away as a new hole appeared in the brim of his floppy felt hat. Bending lower so that his head was almost pressed into the gelding's neck, he kept the horse running hard. If any more slugs sought him out, they were too far away for him to notice or care.

As the horse began to falter, Slocum reluctantly eased back and slowed to a walk. Even this was more than the horse could handle. Slocum dismounted and led the horse off the road into a draw where he hoped he could hide if the outlaws came after him. He sat on a rock, chewed his lower lip, and wondered what the hell was going on. Poking around in the camp for only a few minutes had shown him the Pennsylvania miners had been busy as beavers robbing anything and everything in the territory. The cowboys he had seen the day before trying to move the herd of cattle were others in the gang who had been out rustling.

"Rustling, stealing equipment and stagecoach shipments, they aren't missing anything," Slocum mused. His horse turned a tired brown eye in his direction. He caught the look and read almost human resignation into it. "I know, I know," he said. "This is none of my business."

Seeing the marshal and his posse slaughtered had put him in a precarious position. Luther and any number of others in Sharpesville knew his face. When the marshal's remains were found, he would be the likeliest suspect.

If the body parts were ever found. No one would believe he slaughtered a lawman and six deputies, but as antsy as the marshal had been to string up someone—anyone—Slocum knew anything as simple as the truth was not likely to mean much. The people of Sharpesville wanted a spectacle, and he knew why now.

The wayward Pennsylvania miners, those butchers, had to make life a living hell for anyone living nearby.

Slocum found himself caught between the two factions. The townspeople wanted to put an end to the thieving, and the gang—Slocum was starting to mentally call them the Butchers—wanted him dead, too.

Mounting up and riding like hell was the only way he could see to stay alive. Still, the memory of watching the Butchers hack up the marshal and his posse lingered. During the war, Slocum had seen vicious things, completely cruel and inhuman things. He had ridden with William Quantrill, who had not been a kindly man, driven by utter hatred as he had been, and yet Slocum had not witnessed anything like the scene back in the meadow. Quantrill had ordered his raiders to go into Lawrence, Kansas, and kill every male over the age of eight. Children had been cut down where they stood.

That had been the low point of the war for Slocum, but such savagery paled next to burly men wielding meat cleavers and skinning knives on other humans. Even the Apaches at their most vicious could not compare.

Slocum stood, then froze, one foot in the stirrup. From out on the road came the steady beat of horses' hooves against the hard-packed ground. Somewhere, Slocum had lost his rifle, but he still carried his trusty Colt Navy. He mounted and headed the horse away from the road, following the gentle curve in the draw to get even farther away. Then he drew his six-shooter and waited.

The sound of the horses faded as the riders kept on riding. If they were after him, they had missed his trail when he left the road to rest. Although he had tried to hide his tracks, a good scout would have followed him here.

Slocum snorted in disgust. Those miners might be brutal killers, but they weren't cowboys and they weren't trackers. All their skill came in hard-rock mining—and killing.

Getting his horse out of the rocky draw proved easy enough when he found a segment of the bank that had eroded. He rode straight south now, keeping away from the road. If the Butchers patrolled there, he had no chance of ever getting away without cutting across country. By varying the speed from a trot to a slow walk, Slocum got the most miles possible out of his gelding before it tired too much to go on. He was happy enough with his progress as the sun sank into the west. While he wished it had been a hundred miles, he had probably covered almost fifteen. Unless the Butchers were more determined to hack him apart than he thought, he was safe from them.

It took him the better part of a half hour to make a small fire and bank it so the flames could not be seen from more than a few yards away. He constructed a crude lean-to, more for camouflage than shelter, and only then did he spread out his bedroll. He lay down, found the rocks beneath and tossed them aside, then scooped out the soft dirt at shoulder and hip to make a halfway comfortable bed. Within minutes exhaustion overtook him, and he was sound asleep.

He awoke, hand going to his ebony-handled six-gun as reveille sounded.

Slocum rubbed sleep from his eyes and saw the faint pink tint to the clouds on the eastern horizon. He thought he had been dreaming of his days in the CSA, and then he heard the trumpet sound assembly.

"Damnation," he said, getting to his feet. He made certain his horse was still properly hobbled and cropping grass before he went exploring. After walking for almost ten minutes, he got to a hill overlooking a lush valley.

Smack in the middle of that valley stood an army fort.

He turned to go to his camp, only to find himself staring down the barrel of a rifle. Slocum followed the metal line of the barrel back to the coppery hand wrapped around the stock. A jet-black eye was open while the other squinted at him.

"Mighty hard to miss me at this range," Slocum said. The Indian sighting the rifle at him stood only a few yards away. Slocum judged distances and knew he would be a dead man a couple times over if he tried to run or attack. His only course of action was to find out what the man wanted. "You're Sioux," Slocum said.

He got no answer. Changing tactics, he spoke what few words of Sioux that he knew. This produced a reaction. The closed eye opened so the Indian could stare at him. Slocum tried a few more words.

"I'm not Oglala," the warrior said in English. "And your accent is terrible."

"Your English is mighty good, though," Slocum said.

"Went to mission school. They sent me back East."

"To Pennsylvania?" This produced an unexpected jerk. The Sioux pressed his cheek back into the stock. Slocum saw the man's trigger finger whiten as it tensed.

"Why'd you ask that?"

"Came across a passel of men from Pennsylvania, that's why. Barely got away with all my parts."

"How's that?" The Indian remained vigilant.

"I saw a dozen of them, all dressed in leather aprons, use meat cleavers to kill the Sharpesville marshal and a posse."

"You're not from Pennsylvania." The Indian spoke with a flat tone.

"If you went to school there, you know I'm not. Georgia's where I hail from."

The Sioux nodded slowly as he lowered the rifle.

"You on your way to Fort Walker?"

"That's Fort Walker?" Slocum jerked his thumb over his shoulder in the direction of the army post. "Didn't know the name." Slocum avoided answering directly. "Think they can do anything about the Butchers?"

"You know their name?"

This surprised Slocum. "That's what I called them when I saw how they killed the marshal and his men. Just like a slaughterhouse."

"Most of them were miners back in Pennsylvania. That's what the major's found out. He calls 'em the Schuylkill Butchers since that's where they hail from and that's what they do most."

"Fought around there. Leastwise, to the southwest of Schuylkill Haven," Slocum said. The memory of that bloody fight still burned bright after all the years.

"Gettysburg?"

Slocum shrugged. The Sioux knew a great deal about the area—and he was a good enough scout to come up behind Slocum without alerting him.

"What's your interest in the fort? You a scout?"

"Ever since the Schuylkill Butchers moved into Montana, the major's been sending out scouts to locate them. Not easy. They might be butchers and miners, but they're sneaky. I'm on patrol." The Sioux almost spat the words out.

"Nobody likes being on patrol duty," Slocum said. "Are you going to escort me down to the fort? Or just shoot me on the spot? If you do that, be sure to tell the major where the Butchers are."

"You know?"

Slocum nodded. All he had to do was backtrack on his trail and he would be smack in the middle of the Butchers' camp. Missing all those rustled beeves and stacks of stolen goods would not be easy. The dangerous part was riding through all the outlaws to get there.

"Let's get on down then," the Sioux said.

"You got a name?" Slocum locked eyes with the man.

"Do you?"

"John Slocum."

"Little Foot."

Slocum glanced down and saw the source of the name. The man's right foot was oversized, or so it seemed at first glance, next to his left. Slocum guessed Little Foot's left had been broken and part of it amputated at some point.

"Frostbite. It gets cold in Pennsylvania," Little Foot said simply. He gestured with his rifle.

"No need to keep me covered," Slocum said.

"Nope, no need," Little Foot said, but the rifle did not waver from its bead squarely on Slocum's body.

They walked back to where Slocum had left his gelding. Little Foot let him mount, and then indicated the direction to go in, to where a paint had been staked out. The saddle and other equipment showed that Little Foot was an army scout—or had stolen the gear from the army. Riding in the direction of Fort Walker convinced Slocum he had been caught fair and square by the Sioux scout. Behind him, Little Foot signaled to guards walking sentry duty at the corners of the three-foot-high fence. It kept in poultry and provided a spot for soldiers to crouch and fire if attack came. Otherwise, there wasn't a whole lot of protection for the fort other than the few artillery pieces lined up along the parade ground.

"The major'll want to hear what you have to say," Little Foot said.

"Think he'll keep a gun trained on me, too?"

As if only realizing what he had done for so long, the Sioux scout grinned slightly, lifted the muzzle of the rifle, and motioned for Slocum to go into the commanding officer's office.

Slocum slid to the ground and went to the door, knocked, heard "Enter!" and pushed on inside.

The room was like a hundred other offices he had seen on army posts. It was small, dominated by a single desk in the center of the room, and had a closed-in stench to it. At least there was no trace of anything dying. Slocum had been in some forts where the officers shot the rats from their desks and then left them to rot.

"Who're you?"

"Slocum, and you must be Major Zinsser," Slocum said, reading the name on the desk plate.

"I got work to do. Spit out your business and then get the hell out."

"Little Foot escorted me to the post," Slocum said. He paused when he saw this altered the major's attitude. While not one of respect, at least it was a more polite attention. "I had a run-in with a gang of outlaws he called the Schuylkill Butchers."

"You lived to tell about it? How'd that happen?"

"They were so busy hacking up the marshal and his posse from Sharpesville that they missed me." Slocum felt his jaw tense and his belly knot up. Just mentioning the Butchers sent a thrill of danger throughout his body.

"You know where they are now?" Major Zinsser tried to keep his excitement in check, but failed.

"Little Foot said you've been trying to catch them for a while."

"There's a reward. Hell, I'll pay you out of my own pocket, if that's what you want. Where the hell are they?"

Slocum considered such enthusiasm.

"Who'd you lose?"

Zinsser rocked back in his chair and stared hard at Slocum. "You think a powerful lot, don't you?"

"Keeps me alive. Family?"

"Both of my nephews. My sister Anne sent them out here to become men. They enlisted, and I was supposed to look after them. The Schuylkill Butchers killed them and the rest of a patrol filled with veteran soldiers." Major Zinsser took a deep breath and exhaled slowly. "I found the bodies. The parts of the bodies. I never told my sister."

"Here's a chance to bring them to justice," Slocum said, "but you'll have to commit a goodly portion of your men.

I wasn't counting, but there must have been a hundred of the murdering bastards."

"I've got four companies. One is on patrol down south. Where'd you come from?"

"North about twenty miles."

"A day's hard ride for two companies."

"You'd get there all tuckered out. Better to make it in two."

"You were a cavalry officer? You've got the look and judgment."

"Not in your army."

Zinsser snorted. "With that Georgia cracker drawl of yours, I didn't think you were in the Ninth Maine Infantry."

"You with them when they caught General Johnston?"

Zinsser nodded. "I watched him pass over his sword to General Butler."

"This is going to be a worse fight than Cold Harbor. The Butchers don't have any property to defend. The cattle they've been rustling can be given up in the blink of an eye if it means they can kill an extra soldier or two."

"Dammit, Slocum, I know that. I've tried to catch them ever since they came into this part of Montana."

"What are they after?"

Major Zinsser shook his head, then pushed back from his desk and went to a map on the wall.

"There's a spur of the Montana Northern going into Sharpesville. At least, it'll go there if the countryside's pacified. I flushed out the last of the hostile Indians months back, and that's when the Schuylkill Butchers showed their ugly faces."

"No peaceable land, no railroad?"

"That sums it up. Sharpesville will dry up and blow away without the railroad. With it, the town might become important."

"Right now, they're getting along without a marshal."

"What are you saying?"

Slocum scowled and shook his head slowly. He wasn't sure what he was trying to say. An idea fluttered at the edges of being put into words, but escaped whenever he worked too hard at it.

"You want them caught."

"I want them killed. And it's more than revenge for my nephews. If Sharpesville disappears, so will Fort Walker. There aren't many commands left out West. I'd be mustered out if they close this post."

Everything Zinsser said rang true. Then Slocum broached the subject he had been avoiding.

"What do you want from me? The last I saw of the Butchers, they were camped in this valley." He went to the map, located Sharpesville, and was surprised to see how close it was to Fort Walker. The Schuylkill Butchers were holed up not ten miles from town, but in the direction opposite from the fort.

"You'll lead us," said Zinsser. "Little Foot is good, but having someone who's seen the camp is even better. You can tell us what you remember of the valley and where the Butchers patrolled while we're riding up."

Slocum glanced over his shoulder and saw Little Foot in the doorway, his rifle riding in the crook of his left arm.

"Better get to it then," Slocum said. "I reckon you're going to ride straight through and attack."

"That's the only way to catch them. If they caught so much as a hint that I was on the way with enough troopers to kill or capture the lot of them, they'd disappear into those mountains."

Slocum looked at the map and wondered. Something held the Schuylkill Butchers to that area. He wasn't going to argue with Zinsser, though. It might be for the best if they scared the outlaws away without a fight.

But Slocum doubted that was going to happen. The memory of silvery cleavers and butcher knives flashing in the sun as they hacked at human bodies was too vivid.

5

"Not too far now," Slocum said. He wobbled in the saddle from the all-night ride from Fort Walker, but Major Zinsser looked as fresh as the instant he had settled onto his horse. His eyes were so bright they might have betrayed fever, but Slocum knew better. The army officer had finally found a way to avenge the deaths of his nephews—and probably win himself not only a medal, but the everlasting admiration of the citizens of Sharpesville.

Behind them rode two entire companies of men. The rattle of weapons and the thudding of so many horses' hooves had worried Slocum. Sneaking up on the Schuylkill Butchers did not seem likely, yet they had ridden through the maze of valleys and across broad meadows without being seen. As he had noticed before, the outlaws had nothing but contempt for anyone coming after them. They saw themselves as invincible.

Until now that was true.

Eighty veteran horse soldiers were prepared to change the Pennsylvania killers' lives forever.

"That valley ahead," Slocum said. "They keep the cattle they've rustled at the far end."

"Probably butcher and eat them," Zinsser said. "There haven't been any rustled beeves offered for sale."

Slocum said nothing. He was sure the officer kept a close watch on such trade, but the statement carried more hope than certainty. In these hills, who was to say that a down-on-his-luck rancher wasn't going to buy a few head of stolen cattle to improve his herd?

"Where do we begin the attack, sir?"

Slocum looked at the eager shavetail. The lieutenant was still wet behind the ears. Having a battle-hardened sergeant ask would have suited Slocum more. Looking up, he saw the pale light of a new day cracking open the eastern sky.

"Let me go scout the valley ahead, just to be sure you can get them all on the first attack," Slocum said.

"Take Little Foot with you," Zinsser said. "I'll see that the men are ready for immediate combat."

Slocum knew the men were keyed up and ready. He had seen the rigid way they sat in the saddle, the way they looked around nervously, eyes moving and heads immobile. Veterans they might be, but even going against the Blackfoot or the Sioux had not carried such fear of impending attack. The Indians were hit-and-run fighters. If their initial attack failed, they might try a second or even a third, but eventually they would ride off, whooping and hollering. Even their prisoners were not as badly mistreated as the prisoners of other tribes—like the Apaches. Slocum had seen firsthand too much torture and outright mutilation.

The Schuylkill Butchers were worse.

"They should have stayed in Pennsylvania," Little Foot said. "Not that I wish anything evil on the good people of Pennsylvania."

Slocum wondered how much more about the Butchers Little Foot knew. Going to school in the same state where the Molly Maguires rioted and killed had to bring a bit of chin-wagging his way.

"You want to split up, reconnoiter, then make our way back?" Slocum asked.

"Together," Little Foot decided.

"Why don't you trust me?" asked Slocum.

The Indian turned in the saddle and smiled.

"I don't trust any white man." He looked ahead into the dawn. "I trust them even less. I have seen them."

"You think I'm one of them?"

"They would eat you alive," Little Foot said. With that, he gestured for Slocum to ride ahead.

Slocum did as he was bidden, fuming as he went. Little Foot did not believe he was part of the murderous gang. It was worse. He thought Slocum was a dupe. Slocum might be many things, but that was not one of them. Reaching over, he slipped the leather thong off the hammer of his Colt Navy. He wanted to be ready for anything, even if six shots wouldn't go very far in killing a couple dozen Butchers.

The closer he got to the rise looking down into the valley, the warier he became. Even the Schuylkill Butchers ought to have sentries out. He had seen no one, even asleep, at what should have been a decent lookout point. Little Foot had turned more nervous, too, jumping at small sounds. Killing one or two men on guard would have been normal.

Nothing about this gang of cutthroats from Pennsylvania was normal.

"Down there," Slocum said as they rode along the ridge, hunting for an opening in the trees to get a better view. He heard cattle lowing. Try as he might, he did not hear any horses, though.

"Where are the camps?"

"I see a few campfires," Slocum said. "They've died down."

"All?"

Slocum's heart leaped into his throat. He understood what Little Foot meant. Some of the fires should have been blazing higher than others. A guard would toss a few more logs onto a fire to stay warm. Not everyone in the vast camp would be asleep at the same time. It was as if all the fires had been built and then guttered out over the long night.

"They're not down there," Slocum said.

"We must warn the major," Little Foot said, wheeling his paint about and setting off at a quick trot through the woods on the far side of the ridge. Slocum followed, but his gelding was exhausted after almost a full twenty-four hours of travel. The brightening dawn allowed Slocum to make better time than he normally might, but his horse simply could not be pushed much further without keeling over dead.

He broke out of the woods at the foot of the hill in time to hear a roar go up. It started low and built like the whine of a tornado sweeping across the prairie. Then came the blinding flash of half a hundred rifles firing. Barely had the dazzling glare faded when another volley came. And another and another.

Sporadic fire answered. Slocum recognized the muted pop of army carbines. But there were so few. Too few.

The Schuylkill Butchers had ambushed both companies of cavalry.

"Little Foot!" Slocum shouted. "Little Foot!"

The Sioux scout did not answer. Slocum forced his gelding ahead at the best speed it could muster. But within a hundred yards, he came to the fringes of the massacre. The ground was littered with bright cartridges—spent brass from the outlaws' rifles. They had dug trenches and hidden in them with hunks of canvas pulled across to conceal their position. In the darkness, not expecting such a ploy, Major Zinsser had ridden into a deadly position. From the angle of the trenches, Slocum guessed the entire cavalry detachment had been caught between them.

Once the major stopped to get his men ready for battle, the outlaws had simply thrown back the canvas camouflage and opened fire with their rifles. They didn't even have to be good marksmen to take a deadly toll.

The trenches were empty, but Slocum heard fighting farther on. The Butchers had left the safety of their battle pits and pursued the fleeing soldiers. Or what remained of them.

As Slocum rode, he saw increasing signs of the massacre. Frightened horses. Dead riders. So much blood that the ground had turned into a bloody, muddy paste. Here and there, he saw the signs of the Butchers' special handiwork. An arm or a leg had been severed. But nothing like the slaughter he had witnessed when they attacked the Sharpesville marshal and his posse. There wasn't enough time for that. Yet.

Reacting instinctively at a small noise, Slocum swung about in the saddle and fired twice. A man in a bloodstained leather apron was using a butcher knife on a fallen soldier. Both slugs ripped through the Schuylkill Butcher's head, killing him instantly. Slocum wished he could make the man suffer for his cruelty, but then he saw two more of the outlaws ahead, the morning light glinting off their weapons. He fired at them until his six-shooter came up empty. He might have hit one. There was no way of telling.

What he had done was draw their attention to him.

"O'er here, boyos," called one giant of a man. He waved his bloody cleaver overhead to get the attention of his partners. Then he lumbered toward Slocum.

Reaching back, Slocum slid his Winchester from its sheath and got off a round that caught the outlaw squarely in the chest. The man stumbled and went to his knees, but he was not dead. Slocum remedied that with a second round. By now, however, a dozen Schuylkill Butchers were converging on him. All were armed with knives or meat cleavers. If they had been carrying rifles, he would have been dead in a flash.

Using his knees, he turned his horse and galloped off,

shooting as he went. Mostly he missed, but one round did find its way into a Butcher's leg, felling him amid long, loud curses. As Slocum retreated, he saw the full horror of the battlefield.

He had hoped many of the soldiers could have escaped. If any had, it was only a handful. The stacks of blue-uniformed bodies piled up all around told him how effective and deadly the Butchers' ambush had been. It was as if they had expected the attack. Slocum wondered if someone at the fort had alerted them, or if they were simply more cunning than he had given them credit for. Not seeing sentries did not mean they weren't getting scouting reports from outliers.

When his rifle magazine was expended, Slocum slid it back into its sheath and kept riding. There was nothing he could do for the survivors—the *few* survivors. With any kind of luck, he could circle the battlefield and get back to Fort Walker to tell of Major Zinsser's fate.

As he rode, though, he came across Butchers armed with rifles and pistols. A hot crease along his back warned him he had to be more careful in getting the hell away.

"Thass one. Must be a scout. He ain't in uniform," cried a lookout from high in an oak tree. The lookout bent way out and using a six-shooter opened fire on Slocum. The range was too great, and the man was a terrible shot. Still, Slocum veered away, heading up a narrow valley with a peaceful stream running down the middle of it. Farther down, this stream would be filled with blood. Here, the water looked crystal clear and pure.

From nowhere came two Butchers, one on each side and both grabbing for him. In an instant, Slocum saw they had come from hidden trenches. The Butchers must have cut their defenses deep along every approach leading to their hideout. Slocum wasted no time wondering how long it had taken to dig such extensive pits. He kicked out and caught one outlaw smack in the middle of the face. As the man stumbled away and fell facedown in the stream, causing the very bloody flow that Slocum had thought wasn't likely to exist here, the other owlhoot grabbed and pulled hard. Slocum went flying from the saddle and landed hard on the ground.

He shook off the fall and got to his feet. His six-gun was empty. Reaching down, he curled his fingers over the hilt of the knife he had stashed in his right boot.

The man he faced wasn't the behemoth so many of the Schuylkill Butchers were. He was still well muscled and moved with an easy grace as he waved his long butcher knife in front of him.

"I see I got me a real man fer a change. Ya fight like one with a knife. Now die like one with me knife shoved in yer guts!"

The man rushed Slocum, his butcher knife thrusting straight for the gut. Slocum twisted away at the last possible instant, grabbed the brawny wrist more to get his own balance than to prevent a second slash, and then used his own blade where it would do the most good. His cut was aimed at the man's throat. He got him across the eyes.

"Ya blinded me!" The man lashed out with his knife, flailing wildly. Blood gushed from the wound into the man's eyes. Slocum might have stepped away and left his foe thrashing about.

Instead, he judged his distance, and when opportunity came, he took it. His knife sank up to the hilt in the man's chest, puncturing his heart. The Butcher died way too easily.

Slocum stepped away, panting harshly. He wiped his blade off on the man's leather apron, then went to get his horse.

"Lookin' fer this?" Another of the Butchers held the reins of Slocum's gelding in one hand. In the other he held a six-shooter. "Saw what you done to me friend. Now it's time fer ya to suffer a mite 'fore I slice you up."

The outlaw raised his pistol. The report rang loud and angry in Slocum's ears, but no bullet cut through his flesh.

The Butcher took a half step forward, and then twisted to the ground in a boneless spiral.

Slocum looked up to see Little Foot twenty feet away, lowering his rifle. Smoke still billowed from the muzzle.

"Thanks," Slocum called. "Should we get back to tell them at the fort what happened?"

"You can. I'm leaving."

With that, the Sioux scout vaulted onto his paint horse and galloped away. Loyalty was good only so long in the face of such utter destruction of life.

Slocum took the time to reload before climbing back onto his skittish horse. The smell of blood spooked the gelding and did little for Slocum's peace of mind. He rode directly for the edge of a wooded area, thinking the pine scent would go a long way toward scrubbing the coppery blood stench from his nostrils. When he reached the sheltering woods, he dismounted to give his horse a chance to rest. Whatever happened next, he needed a strong, rested animal beneath him.

Slocum poked through his saddlebags, hunting for what he could count on as supplies. Most of his food was gone. He was down to a single box of cartridges for his rifle. He reloaded the Winchester and took out his field glasses to study the carnage out in the valley. A mist had formed, limiting visibility. There might be rain soon, cleansing rain to wash away all trace of the blood.

Slocum propped his field glasses on a low-hanging tree limb to steady them, and began a slow survey of the battlefield. From what he could tell, the Butchers had crisscrossed the entire area with trenches. Enough of them hiding under canvas in those trenches could ambush a force of any size—and had. Slocum gave up counting the dead soldiers when he reached twenty. Spotting bloodstained gold braid convinced him the major was among the dead.

Little Foot might have lit out for more peaceable regions of Montana, but Slocum knew he had to report this to the officer in command at Fort Walker. From what he could remember, it might be a lieutenant.

That mattered less to Slocum than letting the army know of the danger camped on its doorstep. To hell with railroads and commerce. The Schuylkill Butchers had to be stopped. They were like a plague on the land, moving through and destroying everything as surely as grasshoppers or locusts. The unmoving bodies of so many soldiers convinced Slocum of what he had to do.

Waiting until darkness fell, he carefully formulated what he would report. He had run afoul of the law in Sharpesville because the marshal apparently assumed any stranger riding through had to be one of the Schuylkill Butchers. Slocum had spent the day getting his bearings and deciding on the best route to Fort Walker. Moving through the forest, he eventually came out on the far side close to midnight. The storm he had wondered about earlier finally spattered a few cold raindrops on him. Slocum turned up his collar, pulled down his battered hat, and kept riding.

A little past two, he drew rein and listened hard. The steady drizzle muffled sound, but something was not right. Turning slowly in the saddle, he located the source of the noise. His hand flashed to his ebony-handled Colt Navy, but he did not draw. To fire at the men huddled by the campfire would be suicidal. At least a dozen men held out their hands for warmth. Only the cold rain kept them from spotting Slocum.

He edged his gelding away from the encampment. So many men at one fire meant others were likely near. For whatever reason, the Butchers traveled in huge gangs. He rode at an angle to their camp, only to find the way blocked by seven dim figures, all mounted. As he cut to his left to avoid them, they came galloping in his direction.

As he rode, the rain increased until it beat down at him in sheets of blowing water. Using this to his advantage, Slocum doubled back and tried to get around the seven riders. Rather than continuing after him, hunting in vain, only three continued along what ought to have been his trail. The other four remained as guards.

The way they strung themselves out prevented Slocum from getting around them. His way to Fort Walker was efficiently cut off.

Wheeling around, Slocum headed in a direction that would put as much distance between him and the riders as possible. Changing direction often, he thought he lost them. When he found a road, Slocum looked both left and right, unsure which direction to take. Shrugging off the chance he might be wrong, he turned left and rode steadily. Just before dawn, the rain lightened to hardly more than blowing mist and he saw a sign telling him he was only five miles outside Sharpesville.

He considered his plight. The Schuylkill Butchers cut off any chance of reaching Fort Walker, but if he returned to Sharpesville, whatever deputy had taken up the marshal's job was likely to clap him into jail. They had intended to hang him without a trial. Being put in the same position again didn't set well with Slocum.

But Sharpesville was not far from Fort Walker. Someone in town could get word to the soldiers about their commanding officer and the two companies that had been slaughtered. Duty to Slocum meant more than his life. He urged his tired horse toward Sharpesville.

Barely had he gone a mile when he saw riders ahead, waiting on either side of the road. The rain prevented easy identification.

Lawmen? Whoever they were, they were not heading anywhere. They had staked out this section of road because it was long, straight, and presented no chance for anyone to sneak past without a large detour.

Slocum considered his options. Only four miles outside Sharpesville, they were likely to be lawmen. He took a deep breath, started to put his spurs to his horse, and then stopped when he heard the telltale metallic click of a six-shooter being cocked.

"You don't want to go anywhere," came a muffled voice.

Slocum glanced to his left. All he could see through the undergrowth was the six-gun pointed directly at him.

6

"If you're going to rob me, get on with it," Slocum said, looking around. He felt the Schuylkill Butchers coming closer by the minute. He might have evaded pursuit, but there were so many of them, he could not be sure. "Or you could just shoot me. That'd be more merciful."

"What?" A rustling sounded as bushes were pushed away. Slocum bent low, ready to make a run for it. When he saw whose hand held the six-shooter, he relaxed and sat a little straighter in the saddle. "Why do you *want* me to shoot you? That's crazy."

"Not as crazy as getting caught by a gang of outlaws going by the moniker of—"

"The Schuylkill Butchers," the woman finished. She lowered her pistol and got free of the brush. She came to stand beside his horse, looking up imploringly at him. "You're riding into a dozen or more of them. They're all along the road going into Sharpesville."

"They just massacred two companies of soldiers from Fort Walker," Slocum said, feeling as if he had just upped the ante in a poker game neither of them could possibly win.

"Oh, no. I'd hoped—" She bit off the rest of her sentence. Slocum saw tears welling in her bright blue eyes.

Her auburn hair was in wild disarray, matted and dirty as if she had been crawling around in the forest. Slocum guessed that was exactly what she had been doing. Her clothing was ripped and filthy, and she had lost the top two buttons on her blouse. In spite of her disheveled condition, Slocum could not help noticing, from his position so far above her, that she had a mighty fine pair of breasts struggling to remain tucked into her blouse.

"You thought the soldiers would run the Butchers off?"

"I had hoped they would *kill* them. Kill them all!" She blurted out the words. "They're awful men, awful. Killers, each and every one. They—"

"Someone's coming," Slocum said. "From the direction of Sharpesville. You sure the outlaws are between us and town?"

"Yes!"

He reached down, hand extended. She stared at it as if she did not understand. Slocum bent lower, grabbed her forearm, and yanked hard. She let out a squeal of surprise as she flew through the air only to land hard behind Slocum. The gelding staggered under the double weight. Slocum wasted no time getting the horse headed into the trees near the road. He avoided the thicket where the woman had tried to ambush him, and slipped into less overgrown forest. After only a few yards, Slocum felt his horse's strength disappearing rapidly. He stopped, reached around, and swung the woman to the ground. He quickly followed.

She still held her six-shooter, though she no longer pointed it at him.

"Can you use that or is it only for show?" he asked.

"I didn't much frighten you, did I?"

Slocum laughed without humor.

"Yes, I can use it," she said.

"Why'd you rescue me from the town jailhouse?"

"I heard the marshal say they were going to string you up without a trial because they thought you were one of them."

"The Schuylkill Butchers?"

Her head bobbed rapidly. "Yes, the Butchers. They have been killing and killing and no one can stop them. The marshal thought hanging a few of them—if he could only catch them—would scare off the rest."

"They don't scare," Slocum said.

"I know."

Slocum pulled his rifle from the saddle sheath and backtracked his path into the forest. The horse was not going to carry the pair of them away. Slocum had to let it graze, get some water for it, and then rest. Maybe a day or longer. As he walked, the woman hurried along, struggling to keep up with his long-legged stride.

"I'm John Slocum," he said, forcing himself not to look in her direction. The way she swung her arms, pumping hard, almost running, caused her blouse to gape open so he could see more than was seemly.

"I never introduced myself, did I? But then there was not time when I was hitting Luther over the head. I'm Etta Kehoe."

"Thanks for getting me out of jail, Miss Kehoe. I hope Luther wasn't hurt too bad." Slocum dropped prone to the ground, balancing the rifle on his hands while his elbows dug down into the soft earth. From there, he commanded a long stretch of the road into Sharpesville. Given a tad of luck, he could shoot three or four Butchers from the saddle before they even realized they were under attack. During the war Slocum had been a sniper—one of the best. More than once, he had waited all day long for a single shot at a Yankee officer. Chop off the head, kill the body. While he could never claim his sharpshooting had won a battle, it had certainly done a great deal to turn the tide in the Confederacy's favor.

"Luther will be fine," Etta said, chuckling. "He's got such a thick skull."

"You're Irish," Slocum said, still not looking toward her. Etta had dropped beside him, her almost naked breasts pressing down into the forest detritus. Slocum held back the urge to reach over and brush off the leaves and twigs.

"You said that before, back in town."

"It's true. I hear the lilt in your voice."

"County Kerry," she said. "I'm not like those awful . . . those Butchers. They're from Limerick."

None of that made a lick of sense to Slocum. Before he could get an explanation, he saw movement down the road. He held out his hand to quiet her. Etta saw the riders approaching, too, and caught her breath. She lifted her six-shooter.

"Don't put your finger on the trigger until I tell you," Slocum said. The last thing he wanted was for her to panic and fire a round that would draw the Schuylkill Butchers like flies to shit.

"I won't accidentally fire," she said, peeved. "I know how to use a pistol."

He shushed her again. Two riders halted out on the road, not a hundred feet away. Slocum worried that they had spotted the tracks leading into the woods. The rain continued to fall fitfully. He hoped this washed away any hoofprints, but he dared not rely on that alone for their safety. He got a good sight picture of the man he thought was the leader.

"Shoot!" she urged.

"Not yet. They're waiting for something—someone." Barely had the words slipped from his lips when three more riders trotted up. They came along the road from the direction Slocum had traveled earlier.

"Are you afraid of them?" Etta asked.

Slocum never hesitated when he said, "I'm scared shitless. I've seen men tortured to death by Apaches, men blown apart by artillery, men dying in the damnedest ways you can imagine, and not a bit of it made me sick to my belly like seeing them hack up the Sharpesville marshal and his posse."

"Th-they killed the marshal?"

Slocum settled back down when six of the outlaws gathered in the road, side by side, talking earnestly. Slocum wished he could hear what they were saying.

"Stay here," he said, laying aside his rifle. His quick eyes found low spots and rain-filled gullies he might follow to get closer. Risking his life like this was foolhardy, but Slocum needed to know more about what he faced.

"No, John, wait!"

She clutched at his arm, but he was already slithering on his belly like a snake, finding a muddy notch in the ground filled with weeds and tall grass. He counted on the gentle rain to hide any movement of the vegetation as he worked his way closer. He moved as quietly as any predator stalking its prey, but Slocum knew this would change instantly if any of the men caught sight of him. When he came within twenty feet of the riders, he settled down, letting the grass hide him.

". . . begin the attack."

"Sean says we oughta," another piped up.

"How do we know we won't get all blowed up by that artillery?"

"There's not enough of 'em left fer that," said another. "We kilt half the entire troopers back yonder in the meadow. Another company's out prowling around way down south. There's not fifty men left to protect their fort."

"Our fort," yet another said, correcting him. They all laughed at this.

Slocum realized they intended to attack Fort Walker and kill everyone there. Were the Schuylkill Butchers after the cannon sitting out on the parade ground, or did they simply want to make certain the cavalry wouldn't intrude on their plans?

Slocum waited for one of the men to give some hint of what that plan might be, but was disappointed when they began joshing one another, each claiming to be a better miner than the next.

"There he is," one said suddenly.

Slocum almost bolted, thinking they had spotted him. His instincts took over and kept him frozen in place, not moving a muscle. He let out a pent-up breath when he heard the man say, "There's O'Malley now. Hey, Sean. Sean! Over here!"

Slocum reared up enough to see a red-haired man riding up, flanked by four more men. There seemed an endless number of the Irish killers, as if the ocean had spat out one drop after another and each had formed a ready-made killer on the land.

"What are ya doin' sittin' about makin' small talk, eh?" The one they had waited for had to be their leader. Slocum etched Sean O'Malley's features in his mind. This was the man who approved of inhuman butchery. O'Malley's face revealed none of the cruelty shown by the others, but what murderer's face ever did? Slocum had seen cold-eyed men who bluffed their way in and out of trouble without ever drawing their six-guns. He had also seen men with cherubic faces who would as soon shoot you in the back as talk to you.

"Waitin' fer you, Sean," said the one who had been the most talkative. "We ready to take on the fort?"

"Not yet. We got things to do. You're jist tryin' to worm outta some real work."

"Minin's what I do best."

"And you don't do that none so good," Sean O'Malley said, laughing. "See anybody on this road?"

"We got men posted every half mile or so. Nobody's gettin' in or outta Sharpesville."

"I sent a dozen or two men to keep an eye on Fort Walker, too," O'Malley said. "We 'bout got this part of the countryside all sewed up tighter 'n a shroud."

"Then let's put the lot of 'em into the ground," snarled a dark-haired man who had been silent to this point. Slocum couldn't get a good look at him, but the venom in his words told of anger ready to boil over.

"Patience, Colm, patience is what'll make us all rich

men. Those sons of bitches mine owners back in Pennsylvania will lick our boots when we buy the mines out from under 'em with our money."

"Rather see 'em all dead." The dark-haired man whipped out a meat cleaver and lashed it about in the air. The whistling noise made Slocum uneasy.

"Humiliate them like they done the lot of us Molly Maguires," O'Malley said. "That's the way to get back at 'em fer what they done. Now get on to your posts. We're still huntin' for that Indian scout with the horse soldiers. George and Peter claimed they seen a white man ridin' with the Indian. Might be another scout."

"What harm can they do us?"

"I like to keep things all proper," O'Malley said. His voice carried an edge now. The other Butchers fell silent. "Git on yer way now."

The Schuylkill Butchers turned their ponies and trotted off without another word. For several seconds, Sean O'Malley sat, looking hard at the woods where Etta Kehoe hid. Slocum wondered if the woman had given herself away. O'Malley finally motioned for the bodyguards with him to follow. He rode away, looking back occasionally. Slocum remained where he hid in the weeds until he was sure all the outlaws had ridden out of sight.

Slithering and sliding back the way he had come, Slocum finally reached the woods.

"You're all wet, John!"

"Not easy work getting close to them. Even harder getting away," he said. After spying on O'Malley and his henchmen, Slocum was even more worried about staying alive. O'Malley did not seem the sort of man to do things by half measures. If he thought of sending two men out to hunt for Little Foot and Slocum, he likely had sent twenty.

"We have to get to town and—" Etta stopped when she saw his grim expression. "What, John? What did you overhear?"

"The road between here and town is too well guarded

for us to get there. Their leader, O'Malley, said he had almost as many men watching Fort Walker."

"And? What else?"

Etta was too sharp for her own good. She knew that Slocum was keeping the worst from her.

"He's got a passel of men searching for me and the Sioux scout from the fort. Little Foot hightailed it and won't stop riding until he's in South Dakota. They're never going to find him, but they know I rode with the soldiers, too."

"They're looking for you?"

"As long as you're with me, they're looking for us," he told her harshly.

"I wouldn't stand a chance out there on my own. If you'll have me, I want to stick with you." Her bright eyes welled with tears, but her jaw was firm and set. He had seen determined women before, but never one so adamant.

"What did they do to you? The Butchers?" he asked.

Etta ground her teeth together before speaking. "They killed my family. We had a farm on the far side of Sharpesville. Raised hay and alfalfa, some wheat. We weren't getting rich but we got by."

Her eyes locked with his. If he thought she was determined before, now she was as solid as the Bitterroot Mountains. Nothing was going to shake Etta Kehoe.

"I thought they wouldn't do much more than steal our hay for their horses since we were Irish, too. Pa even spoke Gaelic with them—with O'Malley."

"O'Malley killed your pa?"

"My ma, two brothers, and my baby sister, too. It didn't matter. I . . . I saw what they did to Clara. She was only six, but—" Etta turned white and wobbled. Slocum took her in his arms to keep her from fainting dead away at the memory. He did not ask what the Butchers had done to her sister. After witnessing the way the outlaws had dealt with the town marshal, he could guess that age and sex meant nothing to them when it came to unvarnished brutality.

"I didn't mean to be so weak, John. Really." She tried to push away, but he held her close until she sagged, her face buried in his wet shirt. Her tears hardly added moisture to it, but he knew she felt better for the emotional release.

"Where can we hide out?" he asked. "They've got plans for both Sharpesville and Fort Walker. If we can wait a few days, they'll be busy with other things and I might sneak into the fort to warn them."

"The woods," Etta said, "are not a fit place for man nor beast whilst they are about. They prowl around like wild animals all the time. But we might hide out in the mines in the hills outside of town."

"What of alerting any of the miners?"

"The mines played out a long time back. There's no gold or silver there worth the mentioning."

Slocum considered this and liked the idea. While the mouth of a mine was exposed, entering and leaving were the only times they might be seen. His horse could be left inside, and they could move about freely enough without worrying about somebody spying on them.

"West of town?"

Etta nodded.

Slocum took her arm and steered her back in the direction of his horse. He had started to ask if she had one of her own when he paused.

"What is it, John?" She looked at him with eyes bright and wide.

Slocum shoved her hard to the ground and took off running, dodging and darting through the forest. Behind, he heard Etta cry out. And then the scream was muffled and eaten by distance. Slocum plunged on, angling in the direction of his horse and escape.

7

Slocum heard a final muffled scream from Etta Kehoe, and then only silence. All the animals in the forest had gone quiet, waiting and watching for their own safety. Slocum slowed his breakneck pace and began treading lightly to make as little noise as possible himself. He came to the spot where he had tethered his horse, and saw an outlaw standing with arms crossed, staring in the direction of Etta and whoever had grabbed her.

In a headlong rush, Slocum bent, pulled his knife, and ran straight for the Butcher. The man must have heard a sound that alerted him. He dropped his arms and turned—and died. Slocum lunged with his knife and spitted the man's throat. A bloody gurgle died down quickly as the outlaw breathed his last. Only then did Slocum drop to one knee and gasp to regain his breath. When he was ready, he moved toward the spot where he had abandoned Etta. Another of the burly miners stood over her, working to unbutton his fly.

He died halfway there.

Slocum drove his knife blade into the soft earth and pulled it out. A few drops of blood remained. Once more, he shoved it into the cleansing earth and drew it out, satisfied this time. He put his finger to his lips to keep Etta quiet. She held back her convulsive sobs and hugged herself.

Listening hard, Slocum waited for sounds betraying another outlaw. All he heard now were the chirping birds and small animals moving through the undergrowth.

"Let's go," he said. "There were only two of them."

"Y-you let him—you let him capture me!" Etta Kehoe stared in horror at Slocum. "He would have—"

"They'd have raped you. Then he would probably have carved you up like he did your family."

"How do you know he was the one?"

"I don't. Does it matter? The entire gang's responsible for your family dying."

"You left me to him."

"I had to keep him busy while I scouted out others. There was only one with my horse, but I had to make sure I wasn't facing another army of them." He held out his hand to pull her to her feet. Etta shied away. "Come on. Or this time you'll be on your own."

"You killed another one?"

"Slit his throat," Slocum said. "But that doesn't make us even, you and me."

"What?" The woman shook her head as if to clear out cobwebs. "I don't understand."

"You saved me from jail. These two I killed because they would have skewered me, too. So I still owe you."

Etta laughed nervously.

"I don't really understand the way you think, John."

"No need. Let's ride. Did you have a horse?"

"It stepped in a prairie-dog hole and broke its leg not long before I saw you."

"You put it out of its misery?" Slocum looked at the big six-shooter she had picked up again, wondering if she had done the right thing.

"I did," she said, "but I didn't shoot it. The sound might have attracted unwanted attention from them. I used a rock. A b-big rock."

"Come on," Slocum said, taking her arm and half-dragging her along. "You need to give me directions to the mines. The ones you told me about before." He wanted her concentrating on directing them through the woods and into the hillier country to the west, not dwelling on everything that had happened. More bloodshed would be on its way soon enough, but Slocum hoped Etta could get all this out of her mind before it came pouring down on them.

He mounted and pulled her up behind him. The gelding shuddered under the additional weight, but moved stolidly. Slocum did not push the horse, but let the gelding pace itself. Although it was hardly faster than a walk, they made their way through the woods quickly enough and onto a narrow mining road leading into the hills. Slocum spotted several mines, black tailings spewing from the mouths and down the hillside, but decided they were too close to the main road to afford decent cover.

"There," he said after they had ridden a half hour into the hills. Low mountains loomed in the distance, and these hills were well on their way to achieving that status. Mines had been carved into hard rock farther up the slopes. He brought his horse to a halt as he studied one mine in particular. "That one," he said after almost a minute.

"Why? Is it special?"

"It will be when we're hidden away in it," he said. The horse could not make it up the steep road leading to the mine. He and Etta dismounted so he could lead the gelding up. Once at the abandoned mine, he looked around for signs that anyone had been there recently. He knelt and poked a pile of horse dung. Slocum looked up to see Etta staring intently at him.

"Well?" she said. "Done playing?"

"Somebody's been here within the past week. No longer." Slocum dropped the stick he had used to poke the horse flop and drew his six-shooter. "Wait here. If there's any shooting, get on the horse and hightail it. Don't stop until you're in Canada."

"I won't leave you," she said.

He gave her a cold look that only made her more defiant. He had no time to argue with her. He did not suspect anybody had stayed behind, but whoever had looked at the mine had been here recently. That caused him to become wary. Slocum stopped just outside the mine entrance, then turned and looked down the hillside toward the valley bottom and the twin ruts that passed for a road. Weeds had overgrown much of the tracks. Nobody came this way regularly—but someone had come to this very mine.

Slocum whirled about and plunged into the mine shaft. Less than a dozen paces in, the mine turned pitch-black. Dropping to his knees, Slocum pressed his left hand against a steel track on the mine floor to check for vibration. If anyone moved about deeper in the mine, they would betray themselves if they so much as took a step.

Nothing.

Slocum stood, found a shelf with half a dozen miner's candles, and worked to light one with a lucifer from the tin he carried in his vest pocket. Holding the candle in his left hand and out to the side, he advanced. His keen eyes hunted for any trace that someone had come this far into the mine. Rusted track and a uniform coating of dust told the story. Whoever had been poking around outside had not come into the mine.

Slocum went another twenty feet deeper and found what he had hoped for. A larger chamber had been gnawed from the rock. He ran his fingers over the walls. Whatever the miners had dug for had played out here. The chamber had been dug in all directions hoping to pick up the vein of ore again. That the tunnel ended here told him the mine was played out.

"John? What did you find?" Etta looked both apprehensive and eager when he reappeared outside.

"Come on into the mine. There's plenty of room for the horse. More than in a stall."

Etta followed him back into the mine about ten yards.

There, Slocum turned his horse around so it could look out into the daylight coming in from the mouth of the mine, and took off both saddle and saddlebags. He left the saddle with the horse and slung the saddlebags over his shoulder.

"It's mighty dark in here," Etta said nervously.

"There's plenty of room, and we'll be safe."

"I don't know, John. Something might be hiding, sneak up, and . . . grab you!"

Slocum let out a yelp when she reached around his waist and pulled him back into her. He felt her soft breasts crushed against his back. And then he felt something more. She ran her hands over his belly and worked lower until she cupped his growing manhood. A gentle squeeze made it mighty uncomfortable in his jeans.

"You know what you're doing?" he asked.

"If I don't, I reckon you'll show me different," Etta said. Her fingers never stopped massaging him, pressing and pulling. She continued working on him as he dropped his gun belt to the mine floor. About the same time, she yanked and got his pants down around his knees.

He turned and found she had remained on her knees. Etta looked up at him, her grin broad. She reached out and took him, guided his hardness to her lips, and kissed the very tip. She began kissing and licking all over the plum-shaped tip, and then worked down the shaft. Slocum felt his knees getting wobbly. He reached down and laced his fingers through her auburn hair.

Before he knew it, her lips closed around the end and began sucking gently. He pulled at the back of her head, driving himself into her face inch by inch. The soft lips, the hard teeth, her ever-moving tongue, all excited him more and more until he felt as if he was a stick of dynamite about ready to explode.

"Wait," he said. "No more. Not yet."

"No more?" She grinned wickedly and kept running her fingers up and down his spit-slickened length.

"My turn—your turn," he said, dropping to his knees. Her blouse hung open. The last of the buttons had popped free during her fight with the outlaw. He reached out and pressed his palms flat against her breasts, feeling the soft, pliant flesh crush downward. Etta closed her eyes, threw her head back, and moaned softly.

"So nice, John. I love the feel of—oh!"

He pushed aside the useless fabric and caught the hard little nubs cresting each breast between thumbs and fore-fingers. Tweaking hard, twisting from side to side, he felt her heart rate quicken and her breathing become ragged.

She threw her arms around his neck and leaned forward to kiss him hard. He kept fondling her breasts, stroking over the sleek, satiny slopes, tormenting her nipples until they were rock hard.

"I want your mouth on me," she said, breaking away.

Slocum gently shoved her backward so she lay flat on her back, then gave her what she had asked for. His lips cir-cled around one nip and then the other. He suckled and pressed with his tongue, kissed and breathed hotly on her tender flesh. Etta trembled all over by the time he reached down and ran his hands up under her skirt.

Slowly, thoroughly, he explored the stretch of skin above her knees. Her thighs tensed as he moved from the outside to the inside. Her legs parted for him in wanton invitation.

"You're ready for me," he said. It was not a question. His finger had probed upward and found her hot, wet center.

"Yes, yes, John. Take me. Take me. Oh!" She lifted her behind off the floor as she opened for him. He pushed her skirt up around her waist and moved deliberately. He ached, but was not going to rush this. He wanted to savor every in-stant. He wanted her to share what he felt.

The tip of his erection pressed into her nether lips, then sank an inch inward. He paused, relishing the heat all around the head of his manhood. Then he moved another inch deeper and all resolve vanished in a flash. She tensed her strong inner muscles and clamped down fiercely on him.

He gasped and arched his back, sending himself full length into her tightness. He had intended to make love slowly, taking a long time, enjoying every instant. The sudden pleasure she gave overpowered his intentions.

Slocum began thrusting hard, deep, grinding his hips into hers. For every thrust, she rose to meet him. They melted together and became one, and as one they exploded. Slocum clung to her as she bucked like a wild bronco. For a moment, the world spun out of control around him, and then he sank atop her.

Etta's arms circled him and held him firmly. Then she released him and squirmed a mite.

"Let me breathe," she said. "You're heavy."

He laughed and rolled away. She flowed like liquid into the circle of his arms. In the darkness of the mine, they lay together, saying nothing for a spell.

"I never expected that," she said finally.

"Oh? You thought it would be terrible?"

"No, no," she said, laughing. "I meant I enjoyed it so much more than before. With other men." She tensed. "That doesn't bother you, does it?"

"That you've been with other men? No. Might be a problem if you have a husband out there who's good with a six-gun."

"No husband. Not even a beau. Pa didn't think any of the men in Sharpesville were good enough for me."

"But you found some who were?"

"There was one, but he's dead. The Schuylkill Butchers killed him like they've killed so many others."

"We'll hole up here a day or two; then I'll head over to Fort Walker. From what I overheard, they intend to destroy the fort and everyone in it. I don't know why, though, other than pure cussedness." Slocum doubted this was the sole answer. Sean O'Malley might be a vicious murderer, but he would not remain in the area if killing was all he intended.

"There's a railroad coming into Sharpesville. That might have something to do with it," Etta said. "These mines—the ones around here—are all played out, but with a railroad it might open up prospecting deeper in the mountains. At one time, a considerable amount of gold was taken from these hills."

"Could be, but O'Malley must have something more in mind. He kept talking about mine owners."

"The Molly Maguires were always striking the mines back in Pennsylvania," Etta said. "Those were violent strikes, with both sides losing men from the fights. I doubt any of O'Malley's gang has any love for mine owners."

"It could be they were run out of Pennsylvania," Slocum said. "That would make them bitter enough, but what are they doing here?"

"Killing," she said in a flat voice.

Slocum pulled her a little closer. She lifted one leg and wrapped it around his thigh. Rocking gently, she rubbed herself like a cat against him, but no cat had ever been so exciting. Slocum felt himself responding, and soon they were making love once more. When they finished, Slocum was so tired he could hardly keep his eyes open.

"Ought to spread out the bedroll. The floor's dusty and the rocks are cutting into my skin."

"Into *yours*?" Etta grumbled as she moved around. "I've got stones poking deep into my back."

"Kiss them and make it well?" Slocum suggested.

"My back's not the only place where the rocks cut into me," she said coyly.

"Let me see."

She rolled over to allow Slocum to stroke her, but he stopped when he heard a rhythmic sound.

"What is that?" Etta had heard it, too.

"Sounds like mining. Someone's digging." Slocum sat up, found the candle, and lit it so he could look around the chamber. They were closed off, the only way out back along the shaft where they had entered. He got to his feet, pulled up his pants, and began exploring. Pressing his hand against each wall in turn left him with only one conclusion.

"This way," he said, pointing to the blank rock wall. "Somebody's mining not too far away." The steady reverberation of hammer hitting steel chisel to pry loose ore was too familiar to him to ever confuse with another sound.

"But all the mines are played out," she said. "There's no gold left. There wasn't much to start with, and what was here is all mined."

Slocum leaned against the wall and let the vibration flow through his body. The gold might be gone, but someone was actively working a mine close to where they hid.

8

"What are we going to do?" Etta Kehoe asked anxiously. She clung to his arm so tightly that he felt her fingernails cut into his flesh.

"I have to find out who's doing the digging," Slocum said. He was bone tired, but had no other choice. Better that he find whoever was so eagerly mining than the other way around. "Are you sure these mines don't have anything worthwhile left in them?"

"I've heard a passel of prospectors complain about it. One old miner claimed to have looked in every single mine for pay dirt. He said all he ever got was filthy, and considering how he looked when he thought he was clean, that's saying something."

"Stay here," Slocum said, pulling free of her grip. He drew his six-shooter and started out the tunnel. His gelding snorted in complaint, thinking he wanted to ride again. Slocum patted the horse's neck as he passed, and got a grateful nicker when he stepped past and went out into the sunlight.

Slocum squinted and looked at the sun. He was surprised to see it was nearing sundown. The day had been filled with both danger and pleasure. The danger lingered, and the pleasure had passed more quickly than he would have liked. Not that he was complaining. Any time with Etta was nice. Hours with her looked to be even better.

He swung about when he heard her coming from the mine shaft.

"Go back," he said sharply. "There's no telling who's out in the hills."

"I won't stay there alone," she said firmly. "It's dark."

"Light another candle. There're plenty."

She did not answer. She crossed her arms over her chest, holding her tattered blouse together. The set to her mouth told Slocum arguing was not going to get him anywhere. If she did stay while he struck out to find who mined these old claims, she would only follow at a distance and maybe cause more trouble.

"Stay close, but don't crowd me," he said.

She reached out, caught his shirt, and pulled him back to give him a quick peck on the cheek.

"You're a dear."

Slocum snorted like his gelding had, then surveyed the hillside to find a path through the chaparral and cactus. He stayed low, although he was aware that Etta struggled to keep up and made no effort to present a low profile to anyone on the far side of the valley. More than once, Slocum stopped and pressed his hand into a boulder. The digging stopped and started, as if the miner was checking the ore pulled from the wall for traces of gold. Or maybe he was just growing tired and could not work as hard as he might have earlier in the day.

"Down," Slocum said as they rounded the hill and saw another mine. Outside the mouth of the mine stood four horses. Near a miner's shack, a heavy wagon had been partly loaded with black rock.

"What's going on?" Etta whispered.

"Stay put. I'll be right back." Slocum crouched even lower and made his way to the wagon. He plucked out a fist-sized rock and held it up to the rays of the setting sun.

Then he rubbed the rock across his shirt. It left a dark streak. Slocum tossed it back into the wagon, and had started to return to Etta when he heard men grunting with effort.

He saw two burly men struggling to move an ore cart from the mine. The heavy iron carts ought to have taken both men to push. Instead, each had a cart of his own. Slocum marveled at the strength required to move such loads. They wrestled their loads downhill toward the wagon.

Slocum saw immediately he was in big trouble. The miners were going to dump their ore into the wagon from a flat area just above the bed. If he tried to run, they would spot him right away. Reacting instinctively, Slocum dived under the wagon just as the first cart was dumped over his head. The wagon groaned under the added weight, and black dust settled down all over him. Slocum tried to edge away, but dared not make any noise that would alert the miners.

The second cart was dumped. When he heard the squeaking wheels slowly fade, he guessed the two men had returned to the mine to dig some more. Peering around the edge of the wagon, he saw nothing above. Moving cautiously until he was sure no one could see him, then running, he returned to slide down beside Etta.

"What is it, John? I thought they would catch you for sure."

He tried to brush off the black dust, and only smeared it across his shirt and on his hands.

"Coal," he said. "They're mining coal."

"I didn't know there was any here," Etta said. "No one ever mentioned it."

"The prospectors were all hunting for gold or silver. Maybe tin or copper. There was no call for a prospector to dig away in a coal mine."

"But who—?" Etta clamped her mouth firmly shut. Then she said, "The Butchers. They're miners. The Molly Maguires were all union miners. But why?"

"The railroad's coming to Sharpesville," Slocum said. "It might be they aren't trying as much to stop it as take control of it. If they can supply coal for the steam engines, they can make a lot of money fast."

"But the railroad would have its own supply," she said.

"You've seen how the Butchers work. Any supplier of wood for a steam engine would find himself hacked to pieces."

"But they're all skilled miners. Why kill so wantonly? These mines are worthless to anyone else. They could have worked them like they're doing without slaughtering everyone in sight!"

Slocum had no answer for that. Some men killed because they had to. From what he had seen of O'Malley and his gang, they killed because they enjoyed it. Maybe they had been pushed too far in Pennsylvania and now wanted to take out their anger on anyone crossing their path. Or maybe they had adopted the same tactics as the mine owners in Pennsylvania. Once they supplied the coal to the railroad, they would have a monopoly. O'Malley might see himself as more of a railroad magnate than a mine owner.

"Where else in the area do they mine coal?"

"Why, nowhere that I know. All the railroads use wood for fuel."

"Coal is better. O'Malley is setting himself up to supply more than the spur going into Sharpesville."

"He could never control all the freight moved across Montana," Etta scoffed.

"He might think he can. With a gang the size of the one riding behind him, he just might. Once he wipes out Fort Walker, no one can stop him from doing any damned thing he pleases."

"The army won't allow that. They'll avenge an entire post being wiped out! They'll have to."

Slocum was not so sure. If the Schuylkill Butchers were thorough enough and no survivors carried the tale to the next fort, the army might think it wasn't worth the effort retaking the fort. Since the war, the only real enemy had been the Indians. O'Malley might even convince the army that the Sioux or Blackfoot had been responsible.

He shook his head. Whatever O'Malley planned, it meant the destruction of Fort Walker. Slocum had to warn them.

"Come on," he said to Etta. "I want to get out of here."

"It's almost dusk," she said.

"The perfect time to hightail it. I don't want to spend the night in the mine shaft next over from where four of O'Malley's men are working. Where there are four, there might be forty."

"Where can we go?"

Slocum considered that for a moment, then grinned crookedly.

"Nowhere without being seen," he said, changing his mind. "Let's get on back to the mine and hunker down for a day or two. Might be best hiding under their noses."

"They eat so much boiled cabbage they stink to high heaven," Etta said. "They'd never be able to sniff us out."

"Then you can go wait while I do some scouting, and you won't have to worry about the smell."

Etta wrinkled her nose and said, "You're in need of a bath yourself."

"Might be we can share some bathwater when we get out of here," Slocum said.

"As long as it's hot," she said.

"You being in it would make it almost too hot to stand," Slocum said.

"Be careful, John," she said, turning solemn. "You know how awful they are."

She kissed him quickly and dashed for the mine. He sat by a boulder and waited a spell before going to see if other mines were being worked by the Schuylkill Butchers. He circled the hill in the other direction, and found evidence of new mining activity in two other mines. Tailings from both mines showed the Butchers were mining coal. He trudged on until it got too dark to see, then found a tree and climbed it. Slowly searching the valley for any sign of light turned him increasingly cold inside. No fewer than six mines showed activity—activity he had not seen during the day.

Slocum realized he and Etta had been damned lucky to avoid being seen by the gang. O'Malley had his men scattered throughout the area. Without realizing it, Slocum had ridden smack into the middle of dozens of the killers.

As he edged back around the hill, he heard an odd sound. Cocking his head to one side, he listened hard, but the noise vanished as quickly as it had come. With so many miners working these claims, he might have heard an echo from distant hammering. As he approached the mouth to the mine where he and Etta had taken refuge, though, he stopped, drew his six-shooter, and looked around.

Her blouse lay some distance from the mouth of the mine. Slocum dropped to the ground and studied the prints in the dust. The rocky ground didn't take well to boot prints, but he made out the prints of at least three men—and Etta. Scrambling to his feet, he raced in the direction of the first coal mine he had found. As fast as he ran, he was even quicker skidding to a halt and throwing himself into deep shadows when he saw the blazing campfire.

He had wondered how many men worked this mine. If they had all piled out, he knew. Ten. And trussed up and naked to the waist near the campfire was Etta Kehoe.

Slocum raised his pistol, then lowered it. Even with superb marksmanship in the dark, he could only get six of the men. That left four standing guard over Etta to return fire. He saw all were armed, six-shooters stuffed into their belts. The glint off steel cutting edges came from the side of the fire opposite Etta.

At the moment, they only ogled her. He doubted it would be long before they got down to serious raping. He started back to the other mine to fetch his Winchester. This would even the odds a mite, although accurate shooting was out of the question in the darkness. The best he could hope for was to sow enough confusion that he could bull his way in and rescue Etta before the Schuylkill Butchers realized he was there.

It was a slim chance. He had to take it, or she would die at their hands.

Barely had Slocum gone ten feet when he heard one of the outlaws call out, "Sean! You come to check on us poor rock scratchers?"

"You're makin' the lot of us poor, sittin' about on your fat asses. Where's the wagonload of coal? I got a buyer wantin' it bad."

"Look what we caught," the man said. "Ain't she 'bout the purtiest thing this side of the Emerald Isle?"

Slocum edged back, his fingers tight around the handle of his six-gun. He got close enough to see Sean O'Malley and six more of his gang. Even with a rifle and a couple of six-shooters, Slocum would have no chance of taking them all out or causing enough chaos to scatter them.

"Buck naked, is she now? I like that in a woman." O'Malley laughed. "Throw her in the back of the wagon. When business is done, we'll see about her."

Slocum leveled his six-gun at the Butchers' leader, and then stopped when O'Malley swung about abruptly. His chance at cutting the head off this particular snake had passed. Watching as Etta was lifted and dumped into the rear of the heavily laden wagon made Slocum sick to his stomach. He needed firepower to pry her loose from them.

There was only one place he could find it.

He waited as the Butchers mounted and rattled off down the narrow road leading from the mine. A million wild schemes coursed through his head. What it boiled down to was that getting himself killed did nothing to help Etta. He needed the cavalry.

Slocum made his way back to the mine where he and Etta had taken shelter, hoping that the outlaws had not bothered to check inside and find his horse. To his relief, the gelding was still inside, sleeping after a day of exertion carrying two riders. Slocum prodded the horse to its feet, put on the bridle, and led it outside where he threw the saddle over its back. The horse complained a little, but not enough to balk.

The sky had cleared so Slocum could get his bearings. Then he lit out up the valley in the direction opposite that taken by O'Malley and his men. Pressing his luck, Slocum alternated a canter and a walk to get as much from the horse as he could and still reach Fort Walker quickly.

A little after dawn, he found the road to the army post and went directly for it. Only when he saw three riders ahead on the road did Slocum remember how O'Malley had stationed guards to stop anyone from reaching the post—or possibly getting out.

Slocum reached back and slid his rifle from its sheath as he rode. Riding slowly but steadily as he neared the trio, he waited until he was at the best distance possible before raising the rifle to his shoulder and firing. His shot went wide, but it spooked their horses. He got off a second shot that produced a string of profanity from his target, and then galloped on.

Only when he was twenty yards past did the outlaws open up with their six-guns. By then, hitting him was more a matter of luck than skill. For once, Slocum was lucky.

They came after him, but Slocum bent low and kept riding until Fort Walker stretched before him. O'Malley's three men fell back and let Slocum go. He had caught them napping. Now it was time to rouse the soldiers and get them into the field against O'Malley. It might be too late to save Etta, but it was not too late to bring O'Malley and his Butchers to justice.

Justice dispensed by a blazing six-shooter.

"Halt!" The sentry at the low fence around the fort stepped out to bar Slocum from entering.

"I need to talk to the commanding officer," Slocum barked out.

"Major Zinsser's out on patrol."

"The major's dead. He and both companies with him were ambushed. All are dead. Only Little Foot and I got away."

"You the fella who went out scoutin' fer the major?"

"Who's in command?"

"That'd be Lieutenant Holbine. He just got back from patrol down south."

"I know where the outlaws are. Take me to the lieutenant right now."

"Cain't leave my post." The sentry put his fingers in his mouth and whistled shrilly. "Sergeant Dobbs kin take you."

Slocum saw a portly man with sergeant's stripes waddling out from the direction of the mess hall. From his bulk, the noncom spent far too much time there.

"Gent was scoutin' fer the major," the guard said. "Got a tale to tell on how the major got hisself kilt."

"Bullshit," the sergeant said. "Major Zinsser's the best cavalry officer this side of the Red River. No way would he get himself killed. He had two companies with him to boot."

"The Schuylkill Butchers ambushed him. They're planning on attacking the fort, but you can make a preemptive strike and—"

"What's all this hubbub?" A lieutenant in sharply pressed uniform strode out from the mess hall. Slocum had seen his like before. A garrison soldier and not a field officer.

"You Lieutenant Holbine?"

"I am."

"I need to report. I was scouting with Little Foot for the major."

"Where is that no-account Injun?"

Slocum ignored the man and dismounted. He handed the reins to the sergeant, who immediately passed them over to the sentry. Without caring to see what happened to his horse, Slocum went into Zinsser's office and waited impatiently for the lieutenant. The sergeant trailed behind and filled the doorway with his bulk.

"You are most bumptious, sir, throwing your weight around like this."

Slocum ignored the lieutenant, and began a detailed report on how Zinsser had come to be ambushed and how best to retaliate.

"So, you're saying these outlaws intend to attack Fort Walker and seize it? That's rich." The lieutenant laughed at the absurdity.

"O'Malley intends to set himself up as king," Slocum said. "He gets rid of the army, he cows those in Sharpesville, he runs the railroad that comes into that town, and—"

"And nothing. He can never defeat the U.S. Army." Holbine scowled at Slocum. "Unless I miss my guess, you and your kind learned that lesson the hard way."

"My kind?"

"You Southern crackers."

If Etta had not been O'Malley's prisoner, Slocum would have turned and left the lieutenant and his remaining command to their fate.

"Half your post is dead, chopped up and stacked like cordwood." Slocum felt himself tensing. He didn't bother to describe how O'Malley's gang had hacked up many of the dead soldiers, as if they were nothing more than cattle in a slaughterhouse. "You know how bad it's been around here lately with outlaws. There's only one gang. Zinsser called them the Schuylkill Butchers."

"He did mention them," Lieutenant Holbine said, dismissing the notion with a wave of his hand. "The major is possessed of a fertile imagination. I personally think all the trouble is caused by at least four outlaw bands. It is absurd to think of only one creating such a ruckus. Why, they would have to be organized like . . ."

"Like a friggin' army," the sergeant chimed in. "Ain't gonna see anything like that in these parts 'less it's us."

"Yes, Sergeant, thank you for your colorful appraisal."

"Time's running out," Slocum said. "You were on patrol down south? That means you have two companies left?"

"That is so," the lieutenant said slowly, as if wondering how Slocum might be a spy and for whom.

"Hit O'Malley and his gang hard. Now." Slocum went to the map on the wall. "Here's where they cut the trenches. I suspect they have other traps laid in valleys where the digging is easy."

"Yes, you said they are all displaced Pennsylvania miners."

Slocum ignored the gibe. He traced a line through the hills, past the mines where the outlaws were digging out coal.

"It's too rocky for them to make traps like the ones they used against Zinsser," Slocum said. "If you attack through either of these valleys, you'll catch them in their main camp. It'll be a fight, but surprise will be on your side." Slocum was not sure if even this would work, but asking the pompous lieutenant to send to other forts for reinforcements was not likely to be met with much enthusiasm. Right now, any attack that distracted O'Malley from Etta Kehoe was worthwhile, even if it meant the cavalry would lose a significant portion of the men remaining at Fort Walker.

"I'm sure you think so, Slocum," Holbine said. "Sergeant?"

"Yes, sir?"

Slocum almost cried out in anger at the officer's pigheadedness.

"Take a squad and reconnoiter."

"Yes, sir."

"A squad? They'll be up against a hundred men. More!"

"I'm sure a squad of Fort Walker's finest horse soldiers will suffice against a ragtag band of . . . miners." The disdain in his voice sealed his soldiers' doom.

"I'll get on it right away, sir."

"While we're waiting for your report, Sergeant Dobbs, I'm sure Mr. Slocum will find accommodations here to his liking."

"The guardhouse, sir?" The sergeant grinned ear to ear, showing a broken tooth in front. He turned and motioned to guards on the parade ground. Slocum saw two soldiers come running, rifles at port arms.

"Why not?"

"I haven't done anything but warn you—"

"We'll see what game you're playing and ask Major Zinsser when he returns. Do look for him, Sergeant."

The two armed guards grabbed Slocum and shoved him out of the office toward the stockade. That was the last place Slocum wanted to be when O'Malley attacked the fort.

9

"Sure you don't wanna play some poker?" The guard rocked back in his chair, back braced against the stockade wall. He grinned at Slocum in the tiny cell. "Helps pass the time. I know. I been on both sides of them bars in my day."

"I don't have any money," Slocum said. He looked past the guard through the open door onto the parade ground. The lieutenant had done nothing to move the artillery pieces around where they might be used to defend the fort. Without significant walls or palisades, Fort Walker was easy pickings for a small army of cutthroats like the Schuylkill Butchers.

"Loan you some."

"How'd you ever get it back?"

The guard said, "If I got you all locked up, you won't have much choice, will you?"

"If I'm locked up, how can I make money to pay you back?"

This caused the guard to frown. He picked at his teeth with his thumbnail and finally said, "Don't reckon I thought that through. You got a point."

"I can offer something worth more than a stack of gold

double eagles," Slocum said. The guard looked at him expectantly. "Don't be here when O'Malley and his gang attack. They won't leave anyone alive."

"You goin' on 'bout how the major and two whole companies was killed? I don't believe that for a second."

"When they hack off an arm or a leg, remember I warned you." Slocum rested his hands against the iron bars and shook them the best he could. This cell wasn't as sturdy as the one in Sharpesville, but getting out would be just as hard. He knew Fort Walker had only days at the most before O'Malley attacked.

He had no idea if Etta was still alive. In a way, he hoped she had died quickly. That was more merciful than her other possible fate.

"Somebody's coming," Slocum said, straining to see who rode into the parade ground. The cloud of dust kicked up by pounding hooves veiled the rider, but he saw the McClellan saddle on the horse and knew it was a soldier.

"Yup," the guard said, craning his neck around. "Looks to be Sergeant Dobbs. He's a mean cuss. Don't never play poker with him 'less you intend on losin'. He cheats."

"Find out what hc has to report. Please."

The guard looked hard at Slocum and finally shook his head sadly.

"Now, don't go tryin' to make me leave my post, even by beggin' like that. They might put me in the stocks for a week if I did that. Or if Dobbs took it into that thick skull of his, they might just court-martial me. I don't want to get drummed outta the army. This is 'bout all I know how to do. Why, I was—"

Slocum forced himself to concentrate on sounds from outside the thick-walled stockade. It might have been an approaching thunderstorm, but he knew better.

"They're coming. Do you hear that? Horses. Dozens of horses."

"Must be the major and his men gettin' back. 'Bout right, too."

"Take a look," Slocum said sharply. He had been a captain in the CSA and had learned how to give orders that were obeyed. The guard jumped to his feet, and had his head halfway outside when he stopped.

"You don't tell me what to . . . Oh, sweet Mother Mary!" The guard grabbed his rifle and rushed outside. And died.

Slocum kicked and hammered at his cell door, trying to get free. He was securely locked up. Outside, he saw a dozen or more Schuylkill Butchers riding past, firing as they went and cutting down soldiers who had not taken up their arms. After the first deadly assault, the outlaws jumped to the ground. Slocum closed his eyes and tried not to imagine the sight of knives and meat cleavers being swung. The soldiers they fought now were unarmed.

He shook himself free of the dread and looked around. Getting free of the cell might be possible, given a day or two working on the bars. Slocum had only minutes. Less.

One instant, he had a view of the carnage out on the parade ground. The next, the doorway was filled with a behemoth of a man. The outlaw looked around, then came to the cell and shook the door until it rattled.

Slocum clung to the top of the bars, trying to stay out of sight. For a moment, he thought he had succeeded. The outlaw turned to leave, then spun around and came back, bent slightly and looked up.

"Well, lookit that. I got me a fly on the wall. Or are you hangin' from the ceiling like some kinda spider?"

"Glad to see you," Slocum said, dropping to the floor. "Aieee. My leg. I busted my damn leg jumping down like that."

"I got jist the thin' to fix it." The outlaw found the keys and opened the door. As he moved into the cell, he pulled a long butcher knife from his belt.

Slocum had only an instant to react. He spun around on the floor, kicking hard. Thinking his victim was already injured and not able to put up much of a fight, the outlaw was less wary than he should have been. Slocum's toe looped behind the Butcher's heel. The other foot smashed down on his kneecap. The man grunted in pain, lost his balance, and toppled backward, landing hard. Slocum was on him in an instant. Using both hands, he grasped the man's wrist and twisted viciously.

Slocum drove the man's own knife into his throat.

Panting harshly, Slocum rolled away. The sounds of slaughter across the fort were dying down. The Butchers had killed everyone they could find. Slocum yanked open a cabinet and found his six-shooter, knife, and Winchester. Not much against an army of killers, but he wasn't going to let them take him easily.

He positioned himself in the doorway and studied the carnage. All the sounds of fighting that reached his ears were distant, sporadic—and dying. What bothered him the most was the way a dozen or so of O'Malley's gang went from body to body, slitting throats to make sure the soldiers were all dead.

Slocum raised his rifle and sighted carefully when he saw Sean O'Malley ride to the middle of the parade ground. The outlaw leader held up his hand and silence descended.

"Boys, you done good this day. All the soldiers are gone to meet their Maker, and this is our headquarters now. No more livin' in the middle of a field. We're closer to the mines here and soon enough, we're all gonna be filthy rich!" He twisted in the saddle just as Slocum squeezed back on the trigger. The bullet missed O'Malley's head. For a moment, he seemed not to notice and went on. "We put the coal piles over there."

He settled back in the saddle and looked around. His bodyguards rode closer and blocked Slocum from making a second shot. Ducking back inside the stockade kept Slocum from being spotted. If they had seen him, he would have been a goner. As it was, they only thought some dying soldier had fired a round.

"We need to get the railroad owner to come here so we can . . . convince him."

At this, a cheer went up, followed by hearty laughter. Slocum reckoned the owner would never leave Fort Walker alive unless he gave in to O'Malley's demands. Coal for his engines, possibly a spur to the fort, even a part ownership turned over to the outlaws. O'Malley was carving himself out a small country in the midst of Montana.

Slocum waited to make a second shot, but the opportunity never came. O'Malley rode on, flanked by his cheering men. He vanished into Major Zinsser's office, and the Schuylkill Butchers milled around outside congratulating themselves on murder well done.

There might not be another chance to escape. Slocum slid from the stockade, and dived under a boardwalk when several outlaws came out from the mess hall. He lay facedown in the mud, their boots only inches over his head.

"Hey, we got all the food we kin eat!"

"Better 'n the beeves we been gnawin' on?" someone shot back.

"More 'n just meat. We got flour. We got cabbage! No more boilin' down that skunk cabbage!"

The wood planks sagged above Slocum, pressing him deeper into the mud as more men tromped onto the boardwalk and went into the mess hall. He began crawling along until he was completely coated in filth when he came to the far end of the walk. Slocum poked his head out and chanced a quick look around. He was still in the clear and not far from the stables.

Slocum got his feet under him, and had started for the horses when a cannon discharged. He fell forward, grasping his rifle and wondering if they had opened fire on him. A quick look toward the parade ground showed that several outlaws had fired an artillery piece and were working to fire it again.

Cursing his bad luck, Slocum saw O'Malley and his tight cadre storm from the commanding officer's quarters.

O'Malley went to the men at the cannon and shouted at them. The words came through confused. Slocum realized O'Malley was cursing in Gaelic. Not sure what to do, but knowing something was better than nothing, Slocum walked on, trying not to hurry. That would draw unwanted attention.

He got into the stable and saw a couple dozen skittish horses. Scraping the filth off himself as he walked down the center of the barn, he finally came to the stall holding his gelding. The horse whinnied at him accusingly.

"You've gotten fed," Slocum said. "And watered. I need both." He splashed water from the bucket onto his face and knelt to get mud off his clothing as the stable doors squeaked open.

Slocum placed his rifle in the gelding's stall and slid his knife from his boot top, waiting. The man, tall and reedy and red-haired, staggered in clutching something in his hand.

"Whatcha doin'?" The man came in Slocum's direction.

"Countin' horses. Sean wanted to know what we got."

"Wanna see what I got?" The man held up a severed head. Slocum instantly recognized Lieutenant Holbine and his shocked expression.

The next shocked expression came to the redhead's face. Slocum spun and drove his blade up under the lowest rib on the left side. He didn't feel the tip go through the man's vile heart, but he was still dead in seconds. Slocum rocked back and looked from the bloody knife in his hand to the lieutenant's head on the floor of a nearby stall.

"You fool," Slocum said. Holbine had been a garrison officer. Maybe he had been a good one. Slocum couldn't tell. But he ought to have counted sacks of flour and worried over invoices rather than believe he was fit to command a post. He had paid for his lack of attention to Slocum's warning. Unfortunately, he had sealed the deaths of his entire command, too.

Slocum hurriedly foraged through the stables, stuffing everything useful he could find into his saddlebags. If he got to riding hard, he wouldn't have to stop and hunt for food. He had enough trail rations to put a considerable distance between him and the Schuylkill Butchers.

He thought for a moment, then picked a strong-looking mare to use as a second horse. He could ride until the gelding tired, switch to the mare, and ride until the gelding had rested. By switching this way, he could ride fifty miles in a day. That ought to be more than far enough away.

At the stable door, he looked around to be sure he could ride away without arousing any hue and cry. Slocum froze when he saw a wagon rattling into the parade ground. Lumps of coal bounced out as it came across the uneven terrain—and, still naked to the waist, Etta Kehoe stood in the bed. Her hands were tied behind her back so her breasts were visible to any of the gawking, jeering outlaws. Slocum marveled at the way her breasts seemed lily-white when the rest of her was almost entirely coal-black. Etta tried to look defiant, but did a poor job. She was obviously scared to death at what would happen to her now.

In a way, he had hoped she was already dead. Seeing her alive jolted him into action. He swung into the saddle and judged distances. She could ride the second horse if he raced over, freed her from her ropes, and—

Slocum's plan for a wild-ass rescue died when he realized she was chained into the wagon, not tied with rope. A stick of dynamite would work better than his knife freeing the woman. Looking around, he considered setting fire to the stables. The confusion would draw attention away from Etta. He ought to be able to pull the chains free from where they were fastened into the wood of the wagon bed.

That and a dozen other plans were born and died in a flash.

"We got ourselves some entertainment fer tonight," Sean O'Malley called out. He jumped into the wagon and stood next to Etta. She tried to flinch away when he reached out and touched her sooty cheek, but she was too securely chained for that. "Git on with yer chores. The prize won't be given till midnight!"

Slocum had no idea if he ought to be relieved or furious. O'Malley was torturing Etta with the promise of rape hours later, letting her dread the passing of each second. As much as that was torment for the woman, Slocum saw it as a chance to rescue her. He could never fight so many men. He had thought Fort Walker would provide the soldiers to bring O'Malley and his cutthroats to justice. Instead, the Schuylkill Butchers had bowled over the entire post and now controlled it.

Only one other spot offered enough men and guns to free Etta.

Slocum led his horses out of the stables and around back. He mounted, looked down the road in the direction of Sharpesville, and knew it would be a hard ride. It would be even harder convincing the townspeople this might be their only chance to fight the Schuylkill Butchers and win.

He set off at a gallop, aware of time crushing down on him and the virtually impossible task ahead.

10

Slocum could not do it. He slowed his horse, and finally came to a halt in the middle of the road. Miles ahead lay Sharpesville, but behind was Fort Walker and Etta Kehoe. If he had any trouble at all rousing the men of the town, Etta's doom was sealed. Slocum sat on the unmoving horse and thought hard. What difference did it make now if he got a posse back to fight the Schuylkill Butchers in a day or a week? They had wiped out an entire army post. If they moved directly to Sharpesville, the townspeople would respond.

However, Etta would be dead if he had any trouble at all getting Sharpesville armed and ready. Slocum had no real chance of convincing the new town marshal or anyone else of the danger if they recognized him as the man they were going to hang but who had escaped days earlier.

Reluctantly, he turned his horse and tugged on the reins of the mare he had brought along as a spare ride, and headed back toward Fort Walker. Something would let him free her. If not, he could always kill her before she suffered the fate he knew awaited her. The sight of the woman dressed more in coal soot than clothes, naked to the waist, and heavily chained in the back of the wagon returned to haunt him. Rather than taking out O'Malley, he should have shot her then and there. It would have been more merciful.

But as he rode slowly back toward the army post, he knew he never would have done that then. Now, though, he had steeled himself to drawing back on the trigger to keep Etta from her torture. Better he kill her than let the gang rape her to death.

He cut away from the road and circled the fort at some distance, looking for any sentries the outlaws might have posted. They were still feeling their oats. Slocum had to admit he saw no reason for them to post lookouts. No one knew they had taken over the fort. No one except him, and he had just made the decision not to alert everyone in Sharpesville.

Dismounting, Slocum led his horses down into a gully, and staked them where they could graze on some grassy patches while he went back into the fort. He felt nothing but desolation at the sight of the Butchers strutting around and looting the quartermaster's supply warehouse. From somewhere, they had found liquor, and were well on their way to getting roaring drunk.

That made it easier for Slocum to work his way back to the stables. The killer he had dispatched still lay where he had died. The lieutenant's head stared up sightlessly at him. Slocum wanted to kick it away, but decided against it. The man he had killed would be counted among those who died in the soldiers' feeble attempt to repel the invaders. Unless he showed his hand too early, no one would know he was on the post.

Drifting like a ghost, Slocum checked the armory. It had been the first place the Schuylkill Butchers had looted. He found a carbine, checked it, then loaded it with cartridges scattered across the floor.

A rifle, a six-shooter, a knife—these were all he had to fight upward of a hundred brutal killers.

Slocum thought the odds were lopsided, but he was willing to take the chance to free Etta.

He froze when he heard a stir outside. He dropped to his knees and peered out the armory door to see another tight knot of riders come into the fort. O'Malley left the commander's office and came out to shake hands with the newcomer. The way they stood squared off, eye to eye, looking as if they would go at each other at the slightest provocation, told Slocum there was dissension in the Butchers' ranks. Whoever the man was, he challenged O'Malley—and did so openly.

A scheme came to Slocum as he watched the two. Neither budged an inch. The guards behind each man fingered knives and guns and looked ready for a brawl. If Slocum could take one of the men captive, he might ransom him for Etta. Even better, he might play O'Malley off against his rival.

Slocum sank to the floor and watched as the men finally broke off their staring match. O'Malley and the newcomer went together to Major Zinsser's office and vanished inside. Slocum carefully watched the men still outside. The animosity between the groups was obvious. Freeing Etta might be easier if he could make it look like O'Malley's rival was responsible. How he would do this, Slocum did not know. But at last he had the kernel of a plan. Simply freeing the woman did nothing. They had to get away after he got the chains off her.

Thinking on that, he slipped from the armory and returned to the stables. In the back, a cold forge told where the post farrier had worked. Slocum found a small, heavy hammer and a chisel. These would go a long way toward freeing Etta from her chains.

"Whatcha doin'?"

"Horse needed shoeing," Slocum said, not turning. He held the hammer in one hand and the chisel in the other. He started to put them down so he could go for his six-shooter, but the voice behind him turned mighty cold.

"You move a muscle and yer a dead man. Who are you?"

"I just rode in," Slocum said.

"With Murphy?"

"Yeah, with Murphy." Slocum knew the man's name now. What good that would do him remained to be seen.

"We don't want you and yer boss pokin' around. We took this here fort all by ourselves."

Slocum heard footsteps behind him. He waited for the man to get closer, but something betrayed him.

"Son of a—"

Slocum didn't let him finish. Spinning, he flung the chisel straight at the man's chest. It hit and bounced harmlessly off his thick leather apron. The Butcher hesitated, getting his six-gun trained on Slocum again. This was all the time necessary for Slocum to take a step, lift the hammer, and bring it down smack on top of the man's head.

Slocum recoiled from the blood splattering everywhere. He lifted the hammer, ready for a second blow. It wasn't necessary. The man was dead.

"Damn," Slocum said, stepping away. "I'm no better than they are." He stared at the bloody hammer in his hand and started to throw it away. He stopped. This was the only hammer small enough for him to carry, and he needed it to free Etta. He wiped off the blood the best he could, then tossed it aside for a moment to drag the dead man into a stall out of sight of anyone passing by the open door to the stables. He was getting quite a collection of dead bodies. While they might believe the other had been killed during the fight for the fort, seeing a fresh-killed man would definitely alert them.

If he could have figured how to do it, he would have seen that Murphy and his men got blamed. For all he could tell, one of the Irish hoodlums would look like any of the others. To them, though, there had to be something distinguishing one from another. It might be as simple as a lapel pin or as unfathomable as an accent. For all Slocum knew, they were from different counties in Ireland and instantly recognized the differences.

He tucked the hammer into his gun belt and stuffed the chisel behind him. He walked as if he had gained fifty pounds, but knew he needed the tools. The sun was dipping down, but wouldn't set for another couple hours. Slocum had to act fast. When the bonfires started and real drinking became widespread, Etta would be the prize.

Before he stepped out onto the parade ground to head for the stockade where he hoped she was being held, he stopped. Quickly returning to the stables, he rolled over the man he had just killed and stripped off the leather apron. As camouflage, the apron didn't amount to a hill of beans, but if he could just pass for one of the Butchers from across the parade ground, he had a better chance of success.

It was a faint hope, but all he had. Slocum donned the bloody apron, settled his tools, and then walked out bold as brass and looking like he owned the whole damn fort. Any hint that he did not belong would mean his death.

Slocum got to the stockade and looked inside. The body of the outlaw he had killed had not been moved. All the cells were empty. Wherever they kept Etta, it wasn't here.

The coal wagon had been pulled up at the end of the row of offices where the officers had once run Fort Walker. A shed with a door partially open drew Slocum's attention. He strutted over to it and peered inside. He caught his breath at the sight of Etta dangling from chains. A chain had been wrapped around both wrists and then the ends had been fastened to the shed walls so she hung spread-eagled. Facing away from him, she could not see. Her head lolled to one side.

Slocum stepped forward and then stopped. He couldn't hammer off the manacles without drawing attention. Looking back outside, he saw small groups of the outlaws sitting, gambling, smoking, even fighting. The first sound of freeing the woman would make them all stop and come over to see what was happening.

Etta stirred.

"No, no, don't. Please. Let me go."

He wanted to reassure her, but a guard paced by just then.

"Git on outta there. You know the boss tole us to let her be. She's special."

"Yeah, special. Not for the like of us," Slocum said, keeping his face turned.

"It pisses me off, too," the guard said. "Such a fine lass bein' given to him."

"Murphy doesn't deserve her."

"Murphy? Whatcha sayin'? It ain't Murphy's that's gettin' her. You know that."

Slocum turned, grabbed the front of the guard's shirt, and brought his knee up hard into the exposed groin. The outlaw gasped and doubled over, unable to do more than emit tiny mewling sounds. Slocum brought his knee up again and caught the man on the chin. This knocked him out.

Faced with the chore of getting rid of the guard only added to the urgency Slocum felt. It was as if every tick of the pocket watch in his vest placed both him and Etta that much closer to a violent death.

He considered slitting the guard's throat, then saw a chance to try something else.

Murphy and two of his bodyguards came walking toward the shed, causing Slocum to wonder if the unconscious guard had been wrong. Giving Etta to Murphy as a peace offering might weld the two factions together. Men at the lowest levels hardly ever knew what their superiors schemed.

Slocum rolled the guard out of sight. Etta moaned softly, but did not lift her head or try to look behind her. For once, Slocum thanked his luck. Having her call out his name would have been disastrous. As it was, he had only seconds to make everything work just right.

"Outta the way, boyo," Murphy said. "I want to take a gander at our lovely little bargainin' chip."

"Right in here," Slocum said, stepping to one side. He punched the first guard in the throat. He went down choking on his own blood. The second guard was slow to respond. Slocum used the hammer on his elbow, shattering it. The man's six-shooter fell to the ground as he grabbed his arm and cried out in agony.

Murphy started to turn before Slocum swung the hammer and clipped him on the side of the head. Stunned, Murphy dropped to his knees. His eyes rolled up in his head, but he didn't black out. Slocum quickly moved behind him, drew his knife, and laid it across Murphy's throat.

"Talk fast," Slocum ordered. "Who's coming for the woman?"

"What is this? One of O'Malley's harebrained schemes gone wrong again?"

Slocum moved the knife a fraction of an inch and let the blood run down the man's neck.

"You ain't one of us, are ya?"

"Who?"

"There's no way you git away alive. You might as well kill me."

"I might have a way for you to get rid of O'Malley," Slocum said, taking a wild shot. He felt the way Murphy tensed.

"Now what might that be?"

"So you're interested?"

"He's a soulless killer. I got principles."

Slocum doubted that there was a nickel's difference between the two Irish thugs, but he was in no position to question morals.

"You want what he's angling for," said Slocum.

"You don't have a notion about that, do ya?"

"I'll help you with what I know."

"In exchange for the woman? Now, if I go tradin' her away, what would I use to seal the deal?"

Slocum felt increasingly frustrated. He knew that Murphy was only toying with him now. The man need only spill the details of O'Malley's plan, and they could move ahead. That he didn't utter a word told Slocum that Murphy had recovered his arrogance and feeling of invincibility. He ought to kill Murphy straight out and do something else to free Etta. Every second he held the knife to Murphy's throat was a second closer to being discovered.

"Why did you come here?" Slocum asked. "To Montana?"

"We all got death sentences hangin' o'er our heads in Pennsylvania. Damned mine owners put out bounties on all us Molly Maguires. We could fight, but they got the law on their side. Better to come here and make our own country."

"By killing everyone already here?" Slocum felt Murphy shrug slightly. Death meant nothing to this miner. He had probably seen as many of his friends and family die in the Pennsylvania coal mines as he had from the army soldiers sent to put down his violent strikes against the mine owners.

"They don't mean shit to me," Murphy said loudly. "To none of us. We—"

"Shut up," Slocum said, pulling the knife in to reinforce his order.

Coming onto the parade grounds were O'Malley and three of his men. Those who had ridden in with Murphy all perked up, hands going toward their weapons. Slocum wondered if the big blow-off might be happening.

As if he heard Slocum's thoughts, O'Malley spun and stared straight at the shed. Slocum held Murphy immobile in the doorway, knife across his throat.

"Now what do we have here?"

"Here's your chance," Slocum said softly to Murphy. "I can help."

"Go to hell."

Louder, Slocum called, "I want the woman released and given a horse."

"Do you now?" O'Malley sauntered over, as if nothing in the world bothered him. He stopped directly in front of the shed and tried to get a good look at Slocum. "I don't know you. You ain't one of Murphy's boys. You ain't in uniform so you're not a soldier. What's that make you?"

"Your worst nightmare. I'll cut Murphy's throat if you don't do as I say."

"I can't have that," O'Malley said. "Nobody cuts Murphy's throat because I need him."

Slocum felt a small trickle of relief. He might just pull this off yet, though getting away would be a problem.

"You see, nobody kills Murphy because that's what I want to do myself." O'Malley lifted his six-shooter, aimed, and fired. Slocum took a step back when he felt something crash into his chest. For a moment, he could not understand what happened. Then he saw the hole in the leather apron and knew. O'Malley had shot clean through Murphy, and the bullet had lodged in Slocum's chest. He reached down and brushed at it. He heard the bullet fall to the shed floor. The leather apron had robbed the bullet of whatever killing power it had left after driving all the way through Murphy's body.

"He thought he could run this gang. He's wrong."

Slocum now supported deadweight in front of him, a shield as much as anything else.

"Now, I need to think what to do with you. Are you some Knight of the Round Table, eh? You come ridin' up on yer white horse to save the fair damsel like some damned English knight?" O'Malley fired again into Murphy. Slocum turned slightly, but this bullet did not go entirely through Murphy's body. From the sound, the bullet had hit a rib and been deflected.

"No, no," moaned Etta Kehoe. Slocum started to tell her to get ready. If he could prop up Murphy long enough to get to the hammer and chisel, he thought he could free her from the shackles. Then O'Malley bellowed to his men.

"Git 'em, boys. Now!"

There was no more time.

O'Malley and his gang advanced on the shed, firing as they came.

11

Slocum held on to Murphy until O'Malley was almost at the shed door. With a tremendous heave, Slocum picked up the dead man and threw him into O'Malley's arms. The outlaw staggered back, giving Slocum a fraction of a second to act. He threw his hammer at one of O'Malley's guards and the chisel at the other, forcing them both to dodge. Without hesitation, Slocum whirled about, put his head down, and ran full tilt into the rear of the shed. For an awful instant, he feared it would hold, but the rotted wood yielded and he bulled his way through.

Stumbling, staggering, he got his feet under him as he drew his Colt. Not daring to waste a single shot, Slocum dodged back and forth, then ran straight for the low wall as a few bullets sought his back. When more came, he turned, planted his feet squarely, and fired three deadly rounds. Each caught an outlaw and momentarily threw their ranks into confusion.

He dashed to the wall, vaulted over it, and then crawled fast, using it to conceal himself. There were plenty of the Schuylkill Butchers after him, though. They could split and go in either direction and still outnumber him ten to one.

Then his luck changed.

"What's goin' on?" A sentry sat up and looked around. He rubbed his eyes and reached for his rifle.

"Where's your horse?" Slocum shouted. The man's eyes darted away from the fort. That was the last thing he said. Slocum shot him in the middle of the forehead. Running past, Slocum grabbed the fallen rifle and went in the direction the guard had glanced when asked about his horse. He found it tied to a post oak not far off.

The horse hardly noticed Slocum's weight when he jumped into the saddle. The dead guard weighed a considerable amount more than Slocum. Putting his head down, Slocum turned the horse and got it galloping away. Bullets whined after him, but O'Malley's men were not good shots. That might be another reason they resorted to such savagery. Wielding a knife or meat cleaver was not only more personal, they could be sure their victims died.

Slocum angled away from the fort, got to a rise, and saw a dozen men galloping after him. He lifted the rifle and methodically emptied the magazine at them. He winged one. At this distance and on horseback, he counted it a good shot. Then Slocum rode over the rise, jumped to the ground, and swatted the horse's rump, getting it running like hellfire.

Running along the ridge, he found himself a spot to hide just as the Butchers came swarming over the top.

"There he goes. I see the horse!"

"No rider," said another.

The first outlaw squinted. "He's just hunkerin' down. We kin git him. Let's go!"

Slocum silently cheered on the nearsighted man. The one with better eyesight grumbled but followed, as did the rest. Slocum waited a few seconds to be sure they wouldn't double back, then got to his feet and headed for where he had tethered his horses earlier. They looked up when he hurried to them. Fumbling in his saddlebags for more ammo, Slocum reloaded and then stuffed cartridges into his pocket. Not for the first time, he was glad that he had rechambered the Colt Navy. This let him reload faster without sacrificing the speed and accuracy of the pistol.

Only when he felt he was ready to fight a war did he sit and think hard. What the outlaws did when they finally caught the spooked horse was worrisome, but not as much as how to get Etta Kehoe free. The thought of the woman chained like an animal infuriated him, but when his thoughts turned to her dangling from her shackles in the shed, he also remembered how he had gotten away from O'Malley.

Slocum moaned as pain from a dozen splinters embedded in his face and arms finally caught up with him. Using his knife, he worried out the biggest of the splinters until he bled sluggishly from ten holes in his hide. The rest stung, but no worse than a bee sting. Water from his canteen wiped away the worst of the blood and grime from his face.

He was all patched up, but still faced the same problem as he had before. How did he free Etta? Worse now, O'Malley knew he had someone running free willing to kill to rescue her. Slocum had to admit this might not matter a whole lot to the Pennsylvania miner. Life and death were matters of no concern to him. With Murphy dead, O'Malley might have solidified his leadership to the point where all the Irishmen would follow him.

"I stick my nose in and unite them," Slocum muttered, knowing he might have made matters worse. He had been bold, and it had not worked. He had worked his way through their ranks like an Apache, and that had not worked either. Slocum feared that getting the people of Sharpesville alarmed and into a posse might be Etta's only hope. One man against a small army of killers appeared more and more to be a fool's bet.

He kept returning to how the marshal had tossed him into jail without so much as a fare-thee-well. That spoke to him about the way the citizens of Sharpesville thought. Shooting first and asking questions later was smart, considering the Schuylkill Butchers all around them, but it didn't bode well for listening to a stranger tell them they had to rush out and rescue a woman they might not know that well.

"Back," he said to his horses. The gelding looked at him skeptically, snorted, and then let him mount. Tackling O'Malley's gang again was crazy, but he saw no other way unless he could somehow scrub his conscience clean about leaving a half-naked Etta Kehoe in the outlaws' hands to do with as they pleased.

As Slocum rode in the twilight, he heard the rattle of chains and the creaking of leather from the direction of the road leading to Fort Walker. In need of some advantage, he turned his horse's face in that direction and trotted onto a knoll in time to see a fancy carriage pulled by two horses rolling along in the direction of the army post.

"Hey, wait! Hold up!" Slocum yelled. The driver turned and saw him, then applied the whip to his team, getting even more speed out of them. Slocum knew that the driver thought he was being attacked by road agents.

Cutting across the terrain, Slocum gained a hundred yards on the carriage that stayed on the curving road, but he fell back when a guard with a shotgun opened up on him. Slocum's mind raced, trying to figure how to use the carriage's arrival at the fort to his advantage. The guard would take out a few of the Butchers when they tried to seize the carriage and whoever rode inside, but the fight wouldn't last long.

Slocum veered away and kept his eyes open for more sentries patrolling the fort perimeter. His only hope was that things had remained stirred up among the gang, now that O'Malley had killed his primary rival, and that their lack of discipline would leave gaps in their security.

He slowed and waited as the carriage raced up to the low fence around Fort Walker and then passed through the open gate. Slocum sucked in his breath and held it when he saw that the outlaws did not attack. Instead, they gathered about. From the distance, Slocum could not tell, but thought O'Malley came out to greet the passenger.

He had no idea what was going on. Slocum fumbled in his saddlebags and pulled out his field glasses, but could not get a good enough view of either the man who had just arrived or how O'Malley had greeted him. The way the bulk of the outlaws stood about silently told Slocum more than seeing O'Malley shake hands with his visitor. There was a respect here, or if not that, then tolerance for the newcomer.

When O'Malley and a short, portly man went into the former post commander's office, Slocum slumped. O'Malley had an ally and a rich one. He straightened and used his field glasses to slowly scan the fort. Most of the gang had gone back to the revelry, save for three of them who stood guard at the shed. Without riding around to get a view of the shed where Etta was being held, Slocum knew more of the owlhoots would be at the rear. To get to her now meant killing three—and probably six—before starting to free her from her shackles.

Slocum had come to the end of his rope. He had no idea how to get Etta out alive. Then he perked up when O'Malley and the rotund man exited the commandant's office and walked to the shed. Slocum was especially interested when the guards fell back and even held open the door for O'Malley and his guest. Within minutes, O'Malley came out, leading Etta. From what he could tell, the outlaw had put a chain around Etta's neck and led her like a dog.

O'Malley handed the leash to the man, who tugged and got the half-naked woman staggering toward the carriage. The man got in and pulled Etta in after him. Slocum could not tell if the shackles were still fastened to her wrists, but there was no doubt that she wore one around her neck.

Slocum put his field glasses back in his saddlebags when he saw the carriage wheel around on the parade ground and head out. He waited to see if the outlaws would provide a guard. The carriage had no more protection than it had when it drove into the post.

Slocum's checkered past included more than one stagecoach robbery. Shotgun guards and armed passengers meant little to him if he had a good place to set up an ambush. He galloped back across the countryside, heading for a spot along the road that would be perfect for an ambush. As he raced along through the night, he worried that O'Malley might be using Etta as bait to lure him out of hiding. Such thoughts were irrelevant. Slocum had to try to rescue her.

The gelding's flanks heaved and were lathered by the time he reached the spot where the road dipped down and crossed a wide, sandy arroyo. If the driver tried to rush through this stretch of the road, he would cause a horse to break a leg. The wheels would sink into the gravel and force a slower pace.

Perfect for what Slocum intended.

He dismounted, took his rifle, and found the proper spot. This was no time for mercy. Barely had he settled down, his rifle resting in his hands and his elbows on a rock, when the carriage rattled into view. As he had known, the driver stood, braced himself, and pulled back hard on the reins to slow down. At the precise moment, Slocum squeezed the rifle trigger. The firm pressure against his shoulder went with the satisfaction he had of a good shot. The guard wielding the shotgun grunted and bent over, collapsing into the driver's box.

Slocum stood and yelled, "Stop or you're a dead man, too!"

"You're crazy, man. Don't you know who's inside?"

Slocum fired again, winging the driver. The man had only played for time so he could get his own shooting iron out. He dropped his six-shooter and flopped flat on his back on the carriage roof.

"What's happening? Fredericks? Johnson? I say, what—"

Slocum vaulted the rock he had used as a brace and got to the carriage door as the man thrust out his head. Helping things along, Slocum opened the door and unbalanced the man, who tumbled headfirst to the ground.

"Damnation, I'll have your head for this!"

"Not before I fill you full of holes," Slocum said. He thrust the rifle muzzle against the man's neck and held him down. A quick glance into the carriage showed Etta cowering in the far corner. When she saw what was happening, her attitude changed from passivity to a human cyclone.

She spilled out of the carriage compartment, carrying the chain around her neck. Etta swung the chain over her head and lashed out at the man on the ground.

"Don't kill him, John. I'll do that. He . . . he was going to *use* me! Sexually! They gave me to him!"

He stood back and let her whale away with the chain. The well-dressed man protected his head with his arms and curled up into a rotund ball. He jerked in pain every time she landed the chain on him.

"Hold on," Slocum cautioned. "Don't kill him. I need to know what's going on."

"What's the difference? They—they!" She began sputtering, but the first rush of anger had passed and weakness assailed her. After all Etta had been through, he was surprised she had enough energy to lash out even once with the chain, which was still fastened around her neck. She held the other end of the six-foot length in a weak grip and sagged back against the carriage.

"She wants to kill you. Beat you to death. Can't say I much blame her," Slocum told the man, glancing at Etta and marveling at how good she still looked in spite of her dirty, matted hair and the coal soot covering half her body. She was still naked to the waist, but her firm breasts had somehow been kept clean. They gleamed whitely in the faint starlight. The wild, exhausted, frightened, determined expressions flashing across her face made her all the more desirable. She was not giving up.

"Don't, don't." The man curled up into an even tighter ball.

"Answer fast," Slocum said. "What's your deal with the Schuylkill Butchers?"

"O'Malley and his men? They're from Pennsylvania but—"

"Answer me or I'll just put a bullet in your head."

"No, John, no! That's too fast!" Etta's eyes locked with his. She was going along with him, enjoying the man's discomfort. Slocum wondered if her desire to kill the man had died now, or if she was only recovering her strength before lashing away again. It didn't matter. If it came to it, Slocum would kill the man and lose no sleep.

"Speak up," Slocum said, poking the man with the rifle.

"My railroad. The Montana Northern. We're going all the way to the coast and beating the Northern Pacific. Our costs will be less—"

"O'Malley is selling you cheap coal," Slocum said.

"Yes, yes, we can cut costs by half. He's promised no holdups on construction. We get right-of-way, we—"

"I get the idea," Slocum said. "In exchange for a sex slave, what are you giving him?"

"Land. He wants to forge his own state. Hell, his own *country*! The man's crazy as a loon, but what do I care if I get my right-of-way and beat Jim Hill?" Slocum poked the man with his rifle. He curled up a tad more and chattered on. "O'Malley even promised to make things happen to Hill's feeder line, the St. Paul & Pacific. I can be the first and best railroad north of the Platte."

Slocum took his eyes off the prone man for a moment when Etta shuddered and coughed. This was all it took for the railroad owner to unwind like a compressed spring and kick Slocum in the leg with both feet. Slocum twisted to keep from falling, but did anyway. He clung to his rifle. If he dropped it, the railroad magnate would be on it in a flash.

"He's running, John." Etta took a few steps, swinging the length of chain still fastened to her neck, but her resolve faded after only a few steps in pursuit.

Slocum stayed on his knees, whirled around, and snapped off a shot at the fleeing man. In the dark he had little chance of hitting him. After the report died down, Slocum heard no whimpering or cries of pain. He had missed. Although he might have killed the man outright, the quick shot did not have the feel of a killing shot.

"We've got to get out of here," Slocum said, getting to his feet and grabbing Etta. "Can you ride bareback?"

"I never tried."

"Time you did," Slocum said, working to unharness the two horses in the carriage team. He helped her astride one horse and vaulted astride the other. Using his knees, he guided the horse around, and then walked it away from the carriage to where his gelding looked askance at him, as if saying, "But I'm your horse."

He scooped up the reins and then headed for the small camp where he had left the mare. With four horses, they could make even better time.

"Where are we going?" Etta asked. He told her. "I want to get even with him—with Norris."

"The worm I had on the ground?" Slocum saw how the chain dangled from around her neck, riding between her ample breasts, bouncing gently as she rode. It was not polite to stare, but he could not help himself in spite of everything.

"That's what he called himself. He told me his name was Norris but I had to call him Master." Etta spat. "I'd've clawed his eyes out if he had so much as touched me."

"We can hunt him down," Slocum said dubiously. "This close to the fort and the Butchers, though . . ." He let his sentence trail off so she could finish it in her own way. Too many times he had invaded the gang's territory and come out alive. He had failed to rescue Etta from them repeatedly, and if they got stirred up enough, a hundred murderous gunmen would be on his and Etta's necks. Getting away this one last time didn't look like it was in the cards.

"I want them all dead," she said venomously. "All of them. Every last one of them!"

"There's no call to treat a lady like they did," Slocum said. Etta looked sharply at him, as if angry at his words. Her face softened a mite.

"You mean that, don't you? You are a true Southern gentleman."

"I mean it," Slocum said.

"Nobody's ever called me a lady before. I like it." She looked down at her bare chest. The cold night air caused her nipples to harden. Or was it something else? Slocum could not interpret the look she gave him.

"How far's your camp?" she asked.

"Not much farther. We can—"

"Is it safe there? For a while?"

"You need to rest?"

"I need to forget what they were going to do to me—how they treated me."

Slocum frowned, not sure he followed what she meant, but once they reached the grassy expanse near the maple grove where he had staked the mare, he found out. They dismounted. When he turned, Etta stood directly in front of him.

"Here," she said, holding up the loose end of the chain. The other end was still secured around her neck.

"I had a hammer and chisel to free you, but I used them for something else."

"I don't mind it—if you're the one holding the other end of the chain." She stood cloaked only in starlight when she reached down and unfastened her skirt. It fell softly around her ankles. Naked, she stood waiting for him.

"You don't mind what?" Slocum asked. He held the chain, still not sure what she meant. Then he understood. He began reeling her closer, as if he were pulling a fish onto the bank of a river. Every link that slid through his hand brought her a pace closer, until there was no more room between them. Slocum felt the chain dangling between them, and was dazzled by the sight of her breasts crushing into his chest.

"I'm getting you dirty," she said, rubbing against him and scraping off the coal dust. Her leg curled around his so she could rub her crotch up and down on his thigh.

"I wouldn't want to get these fine garments dirty," Slocum said seriously. His own clothes were as filthy as could be, but he went along with what she wanted because he wanted it, too. Bit by bit, he stripped down until he was as naked as she was—except for the chain around her neck.

"I ought to take that off," he said.

"Leave it," she said. "Use it. I want *you* to use it, John."

He tugged downward on the chain, forcing her to her knees in front of his groin. With only a small pull, her face neared his already hardened manhood. Her lips touched the very tip of his stalk, and he felt a surge of pure fire flash through his loins. Then her lips parted, and she took a bit more of him. An inch. Two. More.

Using the chain, he gently guided her back and forth until her lips and tongue made him weak in the knees. Then she began sucking and kissing the sensitive underside of his manhood.

"No more," he said harshly. "I want more, and you're getting me off too fast with your mouth."

She looked up, her eyes bright in the starlight. Her lips parted slightly, but she did not speak. She wanted him to tell her what to do. She was his slave—his willing slave.

Slocum stepped away and pulled downward on the chain until she was on all fours. He moved behind her and knelt so that her curved ass fit perfectly into the semicircle of his body as he leaned forward. Never releasing the chain, he pulled backward now. She snuggled closer, and he slid easily into her from behind.

They both gasped at the intrusion. Slocum dropped the chain, but neither noticed. Their bodies were filling with stark pleasure and the need for release after all they had endured. Slocum reached around her and fondled her dangling breasts. Etta moaned softly. With his other hand, he stroked over her heaving belly, and went lower until he came to the upper vee of her nether lips. Finding the tiny spit there already popped up and throbbing, he pressed down into it as he thrust a little deeper.

"Oh, John, you fill me up to overflowing. You're so big. Oh, oh!"

He continued to stroke across her breasts and the hard nubs capping each. But the way he flicked his other finger back and forth until it was damp from her inner oils set her off. Etta half-rose, pushed back with her hands, and caused him to sink balls-deep into her.

She began tensing and relaxing her strong inner muscles, and Slocum knew he was reaching the end of his endurance. He wanted this to last, but they had both been through so much. Getting off fast mattered more than all-night love-making.

He began stroking with short, quick moves that built carnal friction rapidly. He had to abandon one position around her body to run his forearm across her belly to hold her close. He pumped with increasing power and need until he could no longer hold back the fierce tide within him.

He spurted out his seed. Seconds later, Etta tensed and cried out like a mournful coyote. They moved together a little while longer, and then he sank forward, the woman beneath him.

"Didn't mean to crush you to the ground," he said, rolling to the side. She got up on her knees. Her blue eyes were like twin stars. Much of the coal soot had rubbed off her body, but patches remained, making her breasts appear whiter than marble in the dim light. But he could not keep from staring at the chain dangling between those fine breasts.

Etta threw one leg over his waist and straddled him. The chain coiled downward onto his belly.

"Go on," she said softly. "Use the chain again. I like it when you're the one holding the other end. I do, John, I do." She reached around behind and ran her hand up inside his thigh until she found his manhood. Clever fingers and a constant rocking motion got him hard again.

He took the chain in his hand and began gently pulling this way and that, moving her around on him, finding new positions, giving them both added pleasure and release.

And then there was nothing left for either of them. They clung to one another as the Montana cold settled down, forcing Slocum to get a blanket. She snuggled close, her arms around him, and was asleep within minutes. For Slocum, sleep took longer. The chain between them made him angry all over again at the men who had locked it around Etta's neck.

Then he joined her in deep, exhausted, dreamless sleep.

12

"Stop Norris, and O'Malley will be stopped," Slocum said, swinging his saddle onto the gelding's back.

"O'Malley is the real criminal," Etta said. "He ought to be hung!"

"I'm not disputing that," Slocum said slowly, looking over his shoulder at her. She wore his spare shirt and filled it nicely. Her skirt hung in tatters, but there was nothing that could be done until they reached Sharpesville. "What is the easiest way to stop O'Malley from getting what he wants? Norris is going to give him money and a hint of being lawful."

"O'Malley," she said firmly. "There's nothing the law would do against Norris. If anything, they'll give that son of a bitch the keys to the city. Besides not having anything to charge Norris with, O'Malley is dangerous."

Slocum saw this was a chicken-or-the-egg question that could be bandied back and forth endlessly. If Norris no longer provided a chance for O'Malley to grab the land and turn it into his own private country, the Schuylkill Butchers would move on. Right now, they were feeling their oats and thought they were invincible. They had wiped out a cavalry troop and seized its fort. They robbed with impunity over

God knows how many square miles of Montana. Something had to be done to bring O'Malley down a rung or two. Slocum knew that, against O'Malley's small army of cutthroats, more than a few companies of soldiers would be required.

"Better to find a lever and use that against O'Malley," Slocum said, swinging up into the saddle. "A frontal assault on the Butchers isn't going to work."

"It must have worked back in Pennsylvania," she said as she mounted. She sat astride the mare he had stolen, thinking hard. With a shrug of resignation that Slocum could not interpret, she looked straight ahead and fell silent. They led the two horses from Norris's carriage, intending to swap horses if theirs tired out too soon. With Sharpesville only half a day's ride away, Slocum doubted it would be necessary, unless O'Malley had sent out patrols to find them.

Norris had nowhere to go but back to Fort Walker. What O'Malley did when Norris squealed like a stuck pig remained to be seen.

They rode at a brisk trot toward Sharpesville, Etta pensive and Slocum alert for any sign of the Schuylkill Butchers. He worried that she might try to take matters into her own hands and foolishly—suicidally—go after O'Malley by herself. He was not entirely convinced that putting an end to Norris's scheme would have any effect at all on O'Malley, but it was something that might be possible. He saw no way to tangle with the entire gang and come out alive.

"There's the town limits," Etta said, speaking for the first time since they had begun the ride to Sharpesville. "I hope you find what you want there."

"It's possible there aren't any solutions," Slocum said.

"That's ridiculous. There is always a solution. You just have to find it." She looked at him, and he almost believed.

"We can get a posse together. O'Malley won't expect an attack on his men while they're at the fort," Slocum said.

Her eyes widened. "You think I'm right?"

"There might not be a way out," Slocum said. "But we have to try something." He snapped the gelding's reins and led the horses down the middle of the main street. The town was strangely quiet for this late in the day.

"Where is everyone?" Etta put his unspoken question into words. "I'm going to find out!"

"Wait!"

Etta was already on the ground and walking toward the dry-goods store. She tried to open the door, but it was locked. Rattling it hard, she finally got a frightened face to peer out at her from inside.

"What's wrong? Where is everyone?"

"Go away. It's dangerous. The marshal don't like folks outside this time of day."

Etta swung about and faced Slocum. They both knew the marshal and his posse—the one intended to bring back Slocum—were dead.

"What marshal?" Slocum called.

The door opened a little, and the frightened man peered out. He wiped his lips, looked up and down the street, then said, "The new marshal. Don't know his name. He . . . he's one of *them*."

Slocum didn't have to ask who that might be.

"Wait here," Slocum told Etta. "I got some business to do."

"John, don't."

He tossed her the reins and slipped the leather thong off the hammer of his six-gun. He had killed a few of the outlaws, but none of their deaths had been all that satisfying. He was not sure this one would be either, but he was willing to find out.

As he walked down the middle of the street hunting for the new marshal, he spotted a familiar face. He walked over to where Luther sat huddled, knees pulled up and head buried as if he could make the world disappear.

"Where is he, Luther?" Slocum asked softly. The boy looked up. His bloodshot eyes were the least of his marred appearance. Someone had beaten him severely. One cheek was swollen and blue with a bruise. The other sported a cut from his upper lip all the way back to his ear.

"It's you? Yer one of 'em. You oughta know."

"The marshal was wrong. You're wrong. The only thing I want with the Butchers is to settle a score." He rested his hand on the ebony butt of his six-shooter. Luther stared at his gun hand as if he had no idea what Slocum intended. "Where?" Slocum asked again.

"Saloon," Luther said dully.

"All right, Luther. Here's what I'm going to do. I'm going to cut down the new marshal, and I want you to organize a posse. We're going to ride to Fort Walker and take on the whole lot of them."

"Ain't 'nuff left in town fer that. Most ever'one's left. I shoulda, but I didn't have nowhere to go."

"How many men are left who can handle a gun? Rifle? Shotgun?"

"Couple dozen maybe."

"You tell them you're the new marshal, and you are deputizing them to defend their town. If they didn't leave Sharpesville, that means they think enough of it and their neighbors to fight."

"Reckon they do," Luther said. Then he locked eyes with Slocum. "It'd be a lie sayin' I was marshal."

"You were a deputy before, weren't you?"

"Well, yeah."

"Then this is like the army. You're next in command." Slocum wanted the young man motivated to organize whoever remained behind. "Get rifles from the marshal's office, and don't forget ammo."

"What are we defendin'?"

Slocum started to snap at the youngster, then realized it was a reasonable question. He smiled and said, "That's up to you. Which part of town's best to defend? They're likely to try burning us out. We can't save everything, but you know best where to fight."

"I reckon I do," Luther said, animated once more with duty as he jumped to his feet. "The far end of town, away from the saloon. If they torch that, the liquor'd go up like a bomb. Better to make a stand at the bank. It's got good walls and—"

"You're going to make a fine marshal, Luther. Get on with your job, and I'll see to mine."

"The saloon. That one across the street. There's only the one of 'em there. That's all they needed after they murdered the mayor and his wife." Luther turned pale. Slocum guessed what the gang had done to the mayor and his family and anyone else who opposed them when O'Malley decided to take over the town.

For a moment, he wondered if it had been O'Malley's doing. Murphy had challenged him for control of the Butchers. The new marshal might be one of his henchmen. Slocum made sure his six-shooter slipped easily from its holster. He didn't give two hoots and a holler which faction of the Schuylkill Butchers had cowed this town. Whether it was one of O'Malley's or Murphy's men mattered less than how many slugs he could pump through his black heart.

His stride confident, Slocum went to the saloon and took one quick look up and down the street before entering. Luther had said one Butcher. Slocum had to be sure the youngster wasn't wrong. And he wasn't. A burly man leaned against the bar, a half-full bottle of whiskey on the bar beside his left hand. On the bar to his right lay a scattergun.

"Who might you be?" The outlaw looked up into the dirty mirror behind the bar but did not turn.

"I'm your guide," Slocum said.

"Guide? What's that supposed to mean?"

"It means I get to show you to the undertaker's parlor to be fitted with a pine box—if anyone wants to go that far. Otherwise, we'll just use your saddle blanket to bury you."

Slocum watched the play of muscles across the man's wide shoulders, and knew he was not going for his shotgun.

"You talk too big to be a local, and you ain't one of us."

"Not a Molly Maguire? Not a bloody-handed killer who butchers women and children?"

Slocum was already going for his six-shooter as the man swung about. He wore a pair of six-shooters thrust into his belt. Meaty hands clutched both butts, but having twice the firepower did him no good. Slocum's first slug caught him smack in the middle of the chest. The second ripped off a piece of ear. Then Slocum began fanning his hammer and sent three of the four remaining bullets into the man's gut.

He was dead as he slid to the floor.

Slocum took the time to reload before going over and kicking the pistols from the dead man's hands. Then he went through the outlaw's pockets and found a wad of greenbacks, close to a thousand dollars. Slocum stuffed it into his own pocket. It was blood money from the citizens of Sharpesville. He could figure out how to give it back to the ones who survived.

If any of them did.

"Y-you git him, mister?"

Slocum whirled about, his Colt Navy leveled at Luther. The young man stood in the door with a rifle held in shaky hands. His eyes darted from the pistol in Slocum's hands to the dead Butcher and back to Slocum's six-shooter.

"What are you doing here?"

"Figgered you might need help. He's one mean hombre." Luther peered past Slocum, swallowed hard, and then amended, "He *was* one mean son of a bitch."

While it hardly improved their odds against the Schuylkill Butchers, Luther's show of support meant he had some backbone. Slocum knew all of the men left in town would have to show the same determination.

"Any others in the gang here in town?" Slocum asked.

"Nope, just him. He was 'posed to keep us in line. Done kilt four men jist fer lookin' sideways at him."

"Have you gotten everyone down to the bank?"

"Some won't budge. Say they'll defend their places theyselves."

"Which ones?"

Luther backed out of the saloon, as if unsure whether the dead outlaw would jump back to life. In the street, he pointed his rifle toward the dry-goods store. "Mr. Rosty there, he won't move. Says he fought the sar."

"The sar?"

"The czar!" came a bellow that echoed from one end of town to the other. "He sent his Cossacks and I spit on them. I spit on these brigands, too!"

"His name ain't Rosty, but that's what we calls 'im. Rostropovich," Luther said carefully, then smiled. "Yep, that's Mr. Rosty's real name."

"Go on to the bank and start barricading the place. Get all the food and water into it you can. Don't forget ammunition."

"Won't, no, sir." Luther took a step, then frowned. "I got one question."

"What is it?"

"What's yer name? Don't know I ever heard it."

Slocum laughed and told him, then went to deal with the Russian dry-goods dealer. It took a bit of argument, but Slocum finally convinced the man to move down to the bank with his wife and three sons.

As Slocum watched the Russian and his family go, he called after them, "Where's Etta? The woman I rode into town with?"

Rostropovich laughed and pointed toward the hotel.

Puzzled by the man's reaction, Slocum went to the hotel and poked his head into the lobby. The curious emptiness of a deserted building greeted him. He went to the stairs and looked up at the second floor.

"Etta? You here?"

"Come on up, John. At the top of the stairs. The door's open."

He went up the creaky steps cautiously, not sure what he

would find. He looked into the room to his left. Empty. He turned right and stopped dead in his tracks.

"Do you like it?" Etta asked. She was dressed in frilly undergarments without a crotch so her auburn thatch poked through a lacy slit in the fabric. Her legs were sheathed in what might have been silk that clung to every contour. As she turned, he saw that the fabric was stretched tautly over her posterior. Etta kept turning and held up her arms. Slocum was again surprised at how he had missed so much with his first look. She wore a blouse that was so thin it almost vanished. It was a white that matched her skin color perfectly, making her appear naked.

She turned this way and that so he could see her profile and her impudent breasts so neatly encased in the diaphanous cloth.

"Mr. Rosty told me to take whatever I wanted. He saw how I was dressed when we got to his shop. He knows there's not likely to be much left when the Butchers find out you've killed the man they left."

"News travels fast," Slocum said.

"I heard the gunfire. I recognized your six-shooter and didn't hear another gun." She continued to pose for him, moving to stand in front of the window. The late daylight came through and set fire to her thin clothing. The gossamer white top turned a brilliant orange. The silk bloomers reflected the sunlight and highlighted the tuft of fur between her legs.

"Oh, you like this? It seems so practical. I don't have to completely undress when I want you to . . ." Etta dropped onto the bed and propped herself up on her elbows. With lascivious slowness, she hiked her feet in the air, knees together. Then she slowly opened them to give Slocum a new and delightfully erotic view.

"We don't have the time," he said.

"Why not? Be quick, John. I want it. Do it fast. Burn me up. I put this on just for you, to excite you."

"Looks like I'm not the only one getting excited," Slocum

said. He took a step forward. Her saw her hard nipples and the way her breath came faster now. Tiny dewdrops dotted her bush.

"Good," she said, eyes half-closed now. She licked her lips. "We can kill two birds with one stone."

Slocum took another step and then hesitated. He looked out the window, swore, and went for his six-gun.

"John! What is it?" Etta sat bolt upright on the bed, her long legs dropping over the side.

"We've got company," he said, pushing the curtain back with the barrel of his pistol. Down in the street rode two of O'Malley's gang. "Get dressed. We've got to get to the bank. Luther's barricaded it."

"Oh, damn them! I'll see them all in hell!"

Etta dressed while Slocum acted. He shoved his six-shooter out the window, sighted, and fired twice. The lead rider fell backward over his horse's rump. The other outlaw went for his rifle and looked around frantically, trying to figure out where the killing shots had come from.

Slocum never gave him the chance to home in. He fired three more times and shot him out of the saddle.

"Why'd you have to kill them right now, John?" Etta settled her blouse and skirt and worked to get into her shoes. "Couldn't it have waited? For a few minutes?"

He wondered at the woman. If they had gotten started, he would have been caught with his pants around his ankles. She had to know he had shot O'Malley's men for a reason. They were going into the saloon and would have found their dead partner in a few seconds.

"Come on. I don't see any more, but they travel in packs like most carrion eaters."

"I've got everything," Etta said, picking up a valise. They hurried down the stairs and into the street.

"I was wrong," Slocum said. "There're more. Lots more." He pushed her toward the far end of town. Etta took off running as fast she as she could carrying the valise.

Slocum worked to reload as he followed more slowly.

He looked up when she suddenly stopped. The carpetbag latch had come open and spilled her fancy new clothes onto the ground. She worked to stuff them all back in.

"Forget them. You can get them later."

"Like hell! These are mine! Mr. Rosty gave them to me . . . for you as a reward for rescuing me."

Slocum bent and grabbed handfuls of fabric and helped her stuff it all into the carpetbag. In a crouch, he pivoted and fired down the street. The range was too great to be effective, but he halted the advance of the Schuylkill Butchers. From this angle, it looked as if a thousand of them had invaded the town.

Etta clutched the bag to her chest and dashed to the bank. The door was locked.

"Let us in!" she called. "They'll kill us if you don't let us in!"

Slocum joined her in pounding hard on the locked door. Then he stopped and faced the advancing tide of death. If he was going to die, he wanted to take a few more of those murdering Irish bastards with him.

13

Slocum aimed and fired until his six-gun came up empty. He grabbed Etta around the waist and swung her out of the line of fire when the lead outlaws opened fire. A hot line cut across his upper arm, and he had to let her go.

"John, you're hit!"

"Run," he grated out. He tried to raise his right arm, and it wouldn't obey. He bent over and grabbed for the knife sheathed in the top of his boot. He could fight left-handed—for a few seconds, until they found the range and even the lousy marksmen killed him.

"No, I—"

Slocum heard a grating behind him as wood slid across wood. Like a mule, he kicked backward and knocked open the bank door. He straightened and fell into Etta. Both of them crashed to the lobby floor. Before he could get to his feet, hands grabbed him and pulled him away.

"Git that there door closed agin," Luther said.

The hands pulling Slocum along the floor dropped him so he could sit up. Etta struggled to roll over a few feet from him. Luther walked forward, rifle in hand, and found a slit cut in the door. He shoved his rifle barrel through it and began firing. From outside came angry sounds and utter confusion. The outlaws had not expected any show of resistance. That they had already lost several of the gang had to throw them into a killing rage.

Luther flinched away when bullets slammed into the door, but he leaned back and peered along the sights and kept firing. By the time Slocum got to the youngster's side, the outlaws had stopped shooting.

"Save your ammo," Slocum advised. Luther turned and stared at him. The boy was in shock. His eyes were glassy, and his hands shook. "It's all right." Slocum gently took the gun from Luther's hand.

"They ain't goin' away," Luther said.

"Thanks for keeping them from killing us," Slocum said. He handed the rifle back.

"Jist doin' my job," Luther said proudly, thrusting out his thin chest. A shiny star glinted on his coat. Slocum slapped him on the back and went to see how Etta was faring. She stood at the rear of the bank lobby talking in a low voice with several women.

She quickly left the women and threw her arms around Slocum's neck, and hugged him so hard that he wondered if she was trying to break his neck. Etta finally released her fierce hold on him but pressed close, her cheek against his chest.

"I thought you were dead out there," she whispered.

"You should have run when I told you," he said.

"If I had, I'd be dead." She pushed away and looked at him critically. "Your arm's still bleeding. Get somebody to help stitch him up. Now!" she barked, as if she were in charge.

"I can help. I used to work with the doc before he skedaddled out of town," said a mousy, brown-haired woman whose eyes never stopped darting around.

"Get to it," Etta said.

"How many are in here?" Slocum asked.

"Four women, eight men, not counting us."

"Fourteen against an army," Slocum said. He had been

reacting to danger, fighting to stay alive, but now he could not summon up enough energy to even rail against the Butchers.

"We can wait them out," Etta said. "Luther did a real good job stocking this place. If we have to, we can hide in the vault." She pointed to the vault door standing open.

"If we go inside and close it, how do we get out?"

"I never thought of that," Etta said. "But if they try burning the bank down around our ears, this is the only way we're going to survive."

Slocum doubted that. He had heard of people trapped in bank vaults suffocating to death. If fourteen of them crowded into that small a space, they wouldn't last an hour. Slocum knew he might start shooting them one by one if they irritated him enough. The wide-open spaces were where he belonged, not penned up like an animal in a cage.

Luther and several men started firing. Slocum glanced over his shoulder to see them at their posts, then winced.

"Sorry," the nurse said. "You moved while I was stitchin' up your arm."

She bit off the thread and sloshed some whiskey onto the wound. It burned like fire and then felt better.

"Thanks," Slocum said, flexing his arm. His fingers worked, and he felt the power returning to his grip. "Let me see what's in the supplies Luther stored for us."

He had not expected much, but when he came to the crate of dynamite, complete with blasting caps and a spool of black miner's fuse, he was impressed. There was more going on in Luther's head than was obvious from his somewhat dim-witted speech.

Slocum completed the inventory and knew they could live off the food for several days, more if the Butchers killed any of those in the bank.

Even as the thought crossed his mind, Slocum heard a gasp and saw a man simply sit down. A stray bullet had come through the loophole in the wall and hit the man in the head, killing him instantly.

"Get him over there," Slocum said, pointing to a spot behind the tellers' cages. "He'll be out of sight there."

Luther and Mr. Rosty carried out Slocum's orders while he returned to preparing the dynamite. He wrapped up two sticks with each crimped detonator and put a one-foot length of fuse on the package. More than once he had worked in mines as a blasting engineer, and he knew the fuse burned at a set rate—one foot per minute.

"What are you going to do, John?" Etta put her hand on his arm. He winced. "Sorry, I forgot," she said, drawing back from his injured arm.

"I need to get to the roof," Slocum said. "Is there any way there from inside the building?"

Etta silently pointed. Slocum saw a metal ring set into the ceiling behind the desk where the president had once been seated, approving and rejecting loans to the citizens of Sharpesville. He shoved a chair over, climbed on it, and tugged hard on the ring. A panel opened and a ladder unfolded. He scrambled up the ladder into a dark attic. On hands and knees, Slocum made his way through the dusty recess to a cantilevered opening at the side of the bank.

He kicked out the grating and chanced a quick look outside. Two outlaws sneaked around the bank, almost directly beneath him. Slocum ducked back, lit the fuse, and waited until it had burned down almost to the blasting cap before dropping the bundle. The two sticks of dynamite exploded above the outlaws' heads. Slocum jerked back as blood spattered upward. He quickly lit another pack of dynamite, knowing other Butchers would come running to see what happened.

A quick look confirmed his suspicions. Four more of O'Malley's gang rushed forward to help their friends. Slocum dropped more dynamite and killed them, too. From behind the bank he heard angry cries and the thunder of horses' hooves. Slocum had done all he could for the moment. He edged back to the ladder and slid back down into the bank.

"What the bloody hell did you go and do, Slocum?" demanded Luther. "Lookee there. You blowed the side off the bank!"

Slocum had killed six outlaws. He had also blown a hole three feet across through the brick wall.

"Plug it up. Use the desk and a couple chairs," Slocum said.

"They kin git in through that hole," Luther whined. "It's hard 'nuff keepin' 'em from gettin' in through the reg'lar doors."

"I think you scared them off, Luther," Slocum said. He coughed and said, "Excuse me. You chased them off, Marshal." This got Luther's mind off the hole in the wall and the considerable chore of keeping thirteen people alive if the outlaws attacked in force. Slocum did not doubt O'Malley would send one of the artillery pieces from Fort Walker to blow open the bank, if the notion occurred to him. And it would, when he lost enough men.

Slocum flexed his stiff right arm until it felt better, then drew his six-shooter and went to the front door. Two of the men looked at him fearfully when he motioned for them to let him out.

"Do you have to go outside, John?" Etta pressed close to him, but did not grab him to stop the reconnaissance. "They might be waiting for you."

"Got to see where they are and how many of them there are. It might be good to patch the brick wall I blew a hole in, too." He pointed to the side of the bank. When she looked, he took the opportunity to slip through the door and into the street. The locking bar slid noisily back into place, accentuating how alone he was.

Keeping close to the wall, he sneaked around the side of the bank and saw the two craters he had blasted with his dynamite. He ignored the bloody patches that had once been outlaws. Around back, he saw where a dozen or more men had waited with their horses. Four of the horses remained, their riders dead by Slocum's hand. He swung into the saddle of one horse and began exploring Sharpesville. The town was eerily silent. If there had been a few of the Schuylkill Butchers left to shoot it out, Slocum would have felt better. As it was, he had the feeling he always got before a huge thunderstorm hit.

The hair on the back of his neck raised, and the silence wore on him. The calm before the storm. Waiting for the other shoe to drop. It all hit him as exactly right.

He returned to the bank and left the horse with the others.

"It's me, Slocum. I'm back. Don't shoot!"

He walked out in front of the bank and stood, hands well away from his six-shooter so the men inside the temporary fortress wouldn't get itchy trigger fingers.

The door opened, and Etta waved him inside. He hurried, ducked through the small opening, and saw two men work to slam the door and bar it behind him.

"The town's deserted," he told them. "But we can't hold out here forever. If O'Malley brings back a cannon or even enough men to pin us here for a week, we're goners."

"What should we do?"

"There are four saddled horses around back. Anyone want to ride out and try to warn other towns? What's the next nearest army post other than Fort Walker?"

"Fort Nealon," Luther said, his face scrunched into a frown of concentration. "Might be thirty miles."

"Forty," corrected another man. "We're better off trying to get to Raymond and warning them."

"Raymond's a town?" Slocum asked. "How big is it?"

"Twice the size of us," Luther said. "'Course that was 'fore we all left town. 'Cept fer us in here, that is."

"We know what you mean, Luther," Mr. Rosty said. "We must ride. Four horses, Slocum?"

"There're more around town, I reckon. Or might be the outlaws took the spare horses. The ones out back used to belong to dead men." His eyes drifted toward the hole in the wall, giving them all a fair picture of who had owned the horses.

"I'll ride to Fort Nealon," one man said. "I got a cousin what lives there. He works for the post sutler."

Three others volunteered, two for Raymond and another for a small mining town up in the hills. The more people alerted to the danger brewing, the better, Slocum thought.

The four took what supplies they needed, then left. Slocum watched as the four trotted out of town, three going east and one westward into the hills. He sank down, back to the wall, and closed his eyes. He tried to remember when he had last slept. The murmur of the others in the bank soothed him, and he had good dreams until he awoke with a start.

"It's Jeremy's horse. The one he rode out on," called a man with his eye pressed to a peephole.

"Where was Jeremy headed?" Slocum asked, getting to his feet.

"Fort Nealon. He had a cousin there," the man answered.

Slocum pulled back the bar on the door and went out. He heard nothing but the soft wind blowing down the street and the settling of buildings in town. He approached the horse slowly so as not to spook it, grabbed the reins, and pulled its head down.

Long smears of blood had dried on the horse's mane. Slocum ran his fingers gently along the bloodied hair, looking for the wound. The horse tried to rear, but Slocum held it down. Nowhere did he find a cut on the horse. The blood had to belong to Jeremy. From the amount already dried on the horse, Slocum doubted the rider could have survived.

He led the horse around back and tethered it.

As he went into the street in front of the bank, he heard the pounding of hooves. He spun, went into a crouch, and had his Colt Navy out in a flash. Three more horses galloped past. It wasn't hard to identify them. They had all carried riders out to raise the alarm. O'Malley had bottled up Sharpesville and wasn't allowing anyone to escape.

Slocum rapped sharply on the door and bellowed, "Let me in. Now!"

The door opened a crack and Slocum pushed through, sending Mr. Rosty stumbling back.

"Sorry," Slocum said. "We got big problems." The rest of them gathered around looking fearful. He knew they had no choice but to fight for their lives now, and he did not want any of them simply giving up. That would be suicide.

"They didn't make it, did they?" Etta asked.

"All four of them were killed or caught by O'Malley's gang," Slocum said. There was no reason to sugarcoat the truth. "If we don't get help, they'll wear us down or blow us up. Anybody have any suggestions before they decide to hit us with another frontal assault?"

A weedy man squinted at Slocum through thick glasses and tentatively raised his hand.

"This isn't a schoolroom. Speak up if you have any ideas."

"I'm the town telegrapher. We might get a 'gram out. Sending it along, every telegrapher on the route would hear it."

"You mean send it to someplace far away like Billings and let the message be read as it goes?" Etta sounded outraged that anyone listened in on such communication.

"Ma'am," the telegrapher said, "none of us can help but hear. It makes our jobs a little less boring, too. No safer." He held up his arms. He wore heavy leather forearm protectors. From the burns on his hands, Slocum guessed the reason. The dangerous acid used in the batteries splattered everywhere. He had seen more than one telegrapher who had gone blind from the fumes.

"Where's the telegraph office?" Slocum asked.

"Right down the street, not fifty yards off," the man said.

"Let's go. What's the farthest you can send a telegram?"

"Why, all the way to New York City. With luck I can get a 'gram to Paris, France, but they wouldn't be much help.

Better to just send out a warning. Our only line's between here 'n Miles City. From there the telegrapher would have to repeat the message."

"That's good enough," Slocum said. He motioned for the gatekeepers to open once more. Slocum wondered how many more times they would let him back in before deciding he was a liability rather than an asset. Every time he spoke, he gave them more bad news.

Then he realized Luther wasn't going to let them keep him locked out. Between him and Etta, they would have a pair of tornadoes blowing through the bank. That made him feel a little better, but did nothing to allay his fear about what O'Malley would do next.

Slocum and the telegrapher hurried down the dusty street to the telegraph office. The man fumbled in his vest pocket and took out a key. He had trouble with it in the lock. Slocum pushed him aside, kicked open the door, and then entered.

"That's Western Union property!" the telegrapher protested.

"Bill me," Slocum said. He was in no mood to waste time.

"Very well, I shall do that," the man said primly. He put on his green eyeshade, went around the counter, and sat before the complicated box holding contacts and levers. Dextrous fingers connected copper wires to shiny terminals, and then he poured sulfuric acid into the lead-acid battery at his feet. "It'll take a few seconds to get up to snuff. There." He cracked his knuckles and looked up expectantly at Slocum. "What do I send?"

"Sharpesville attacked. Fort Walker overrun. All dead. Send help."

"Should I make that 'lots of help'?"

"Do it that way," Slocum said. The message wording was less important than alerting the authorities all around to the danger. Let them think it was Indians. Whatever got the most soldiers out to investigate was the best message possible.

"Hmmm," the telegrapher said, frowning. He worked a few seconds on the wires wrapped around brass posts, then worked on his key again. The clicking of the message being sent in Morse code sounded flat to Slocum. He had heard enough telegrams being keyed to know something was wrong.

"Why isn't the message going out?"

"Well, my equipment's in good condition. There's a spark. See?" The telegrapher held a small brass rod across two contacts and caused a fat blue spark to jump and crackle. "That can mean only one thing."

Slocum knew what it was.

"The Butchers have cut the line," he said.

They were isolated and sitting ducks for O'Malley's attack.

14

Slocum fumed as the telegrapher worked on his rig and finally shook his head.

"No question 'bout it," he said. "The line's been cut somewhere between here and Miles City. It happens, though not this time of year so much. Ice gets on the wire and—"

"O'Malley's men cut it," Slocum said flatly. He looked hard at the telegrapher. "If I splice the line, could you get the message through?"

"Of course, but I'd have to know when you fixed the line. And then there's the problem of the outlaws. If they cut the line in one place, they might do it in two or a dozen. All it'd take to bring it down is a long piece of rope with heavy rocks tied on each end." The telegrapher stood and acted out the process of throwing the rope upward, over the telegraph wire, and everything crashing to earth.

"Any way of knowing how far from town they cut the line?" Slocum asked. He rummaged through the telegrapher's tools, taking out a spool of heavy, insulated wire.

"No way I ever heard. Thought on it myself, though. Having a cut wire's like walking into a wall. I mean, you don't go farther and neither does the signal. How far back you stumble from the wall tells you where the wall is. I reckon it'd be possible to time how long it took the signal to hit the cut and get back to me if you knew how fast the message went. Nobody's fer certain sure on that, but it might be really fast. As fast as a hundred miles an hour maybe."

"So? Where's the cut?"

"I said it ought to be possible. I don't know any way of actually *doing* it, other than to ride the line and hunt for where the wire's down."

"Keep sending the signal every ten minutes or so," Slocum said. He glanced at the huge Regulator clock on the wall balefully ticking off every second. "No need to start for a half hour or so. It'll take at least that long for me to find the cut and do the splicing."

"Sounds like you done this before. You know how to prepare the wire?"

Slocum nodded. Other than knowing the code used to send the telegrams, he probably knew more about setting up and repairing a telegraphy shop than this man did. He had not spent all his time out West punching cattle, though that appealed to him more by the minute.

He hunted for his gelding, found it alongside the mare that had carried Etta so ably from Fort Walker, and wasted no time getting on the road. The telegraph poles were visible even if the wire sometimes vanished against the increasingly cloudy sky. The gray storm clouds gathering often blended with the insulating wire. He rode at a brisk trot, then slowed and looked behind him at the wire.

He was less than a mile out of town, but something did not set right with him. Slocum retraced his route, riding directly under the wire rather than simply looking at it from the road. By staring straight up at it, he found a white cloud to use as a contrasting background. A slow smile came to his lips.

"I'll be damned, but I am lucky," he said. The stretch of telegraph line above his head showed brown, while on either side it was a sticky black. Slocum had seen how Apaches sometimes cut telegraph lines, but held the ends together using rawhide strips. Finding the dangling wire and repairing it was easy. That sort of damage happened all the time, usually from natural causes. But if the line was still strung overhead, finding the cut and fixing it took added skill.

Or luck.

Slocum decided in this case it was better to have been lucky than skillful. Something about the way this section of the line dangled farther down had worried at him enough to look at it again.

"Sean O'Malley, you're one sneaky bastard," Slocum said as he dismounted and dropped the spool of wire to the ground.

A proper repair job would have required him to string the new wire up high to keep animals from gnawing on it. Slocum had no reason to be so painstaking. He cut a length of rope from his lariat, went to one telegraph pole and looped it around, then tied it to his waist. Using this as a support, he worked his way up the pole until he got to the glass insulator. Taking a deep breath, Slocum gripped the wire and leaned out as far as he could before tugging hard. The rawhide strip the outlaws had used to fasten the wire where they had cut it parted.

He lost his balance, and flailed about, glad he still had the rope around his middle to keep from falling. Slocum then shinnied down the pole and went to the two ends of the wire lying on the ground some ten feet apart.

Running his fingers over one end showed he was right. The Butchers had slashed through the wire with something sharp. He shivered, knowing that same cleaver had probably dismembered a human or two. Using his own knife, he scraped the insulation away and worked on the copper wire itself until it was bright. Taking one end of the wire from his spool, he spiraled it around a few times and bent it back, making a crude but serviceable connection.

He went to the other dangling wire and repeated the process, using the other end of the wire on his spool. Slocum had been gone for more than an hour. He hoped the telegrapher was following his orders to send a message every few minutes. The wire lay on the ground. Tentatively touching one of the bare connections, Slocum hoped to feel an electric jolt. Nothing. Either the telegrapher was not sending, or there wouldn't be an electric spark. He didn't know enough about these things to figure out what was—or wasn't—happening.

Slocum stepped away and knew there might be another reason he felt nothing. This might not be the only spot the Butchers had cut the telegraph line. He had found it mostly by luck, but with the sun setting, he had no chance at all of seeing the color difference between rawhide and insulation in the dark.

Mounted, Slocum stared at the wire laid along the ground and hoped the message had gotten through to Miles City. If the cavalry couldn't come, he hoped a federal marshal and a posse big enough to matter did.

He swung around and headed back for Sharpesville. Barely a quarter mile toward the town, he saw movement along the road that caused him to stop and wait. He was partially hidden in the twilight, but still silhouetted by the evening sky glow. Urging his horse sideways, he got off the road to a spot where a grove of maples hid him fairly well. Doing nothing for several minutes allowed him to see how antsy the men along the road were. All they could do was lie doggo for a few seconds, then move around rustling the shrubs and disturbing the animals. The normal night sounds were absent. That alone would alert anyone on the road paying attention.

If the silence did not warn a rider, the constant movement would. Slocum counted five men in hiding.

Taking them out would be quite a chore since three of them were bunched together on the far side of the road. The ones on his side had separated by twenty yards. A quiet kill was possible on each of them.

"What do I do about the three sitting together behind that chokeberry bush?" he mused out loud. He had no easy answer. What worried him more than killing the five was where they had come from. The terrain on either side of the road was mostly thicket. While he had been occupied splicing the telegraph line, he would have heard something of them moving into ambush position alongside the road.

They hadn't come from the direction Slocum had headed in his search for the break. That meant they had come from town.

His heart beat faster. He took a deep breath and caught the scent of burning wood. Mixed with it were odors he could not recognize. Even worse, as he watched above the trees, a faint flickering orange showed from the direction of Sharpesville.

The Schuylkill Butchers had attacked after he left and had set fire to the town.

Slocum gently turned his horse away from the road, and made his way through the very thicket that would have alerted him of the outlaws' presence. He made some noise pressing through the undergrowth, but he heard nothing to tell him the men along the road noticed or much cared. For all they knew, he could be another of their gang.

Riding in a wide half circle, Slocum took almost an hour to get back to Sharpesville. The closer he got, the stronger was the acrid stench of burning wood. He felt the heat on his face by the time he came out of the woods just behind the town. If anything remained of the town, he was hard-pressed to figure what it was. His gelding turned skittish at the sight of the flames, now dying down. He kept firm control and worked his way along to the far end of town and the bank.

Being made of brick, it had not burned. The roof had collapsed, though. If anyone had been inside, they could not have survived.

"Etta," he said in a cold, grim tone. He found a spot a hundred yards away to tether his horse so he could scout on foot. The flames had died down there, leaving the remnants of the buildings sooty and barren. Poking through a couple structures near the bank did nothing to bolster his optimism. By the time he worked through the hole in the bank wall, he knew no one could be alive.

Using a charred timber, he pushed away fallen beams and bricks from half a dozen bodies. The stench almost made him gag, but he examined each body in turn. Slocum wasn't sure if he hoped he'd find Etta's corpse or not.

In a way, it would be a fitting end if she had perished in the blaze. Her misery would have ended. If she had escaped the fire, he doubted she had eluded the Schuylkill Butchers. Being their prisoner again would be far worse than dying.

Twenty minutes of sifting through the debris produced no other bodies. He had not found Etta Kehoe. He took a deep breath, choked on the smoke, then threw down the timber he had used as a fireplace poker. One more place had to be checked before he figured out what to do next.

Cautiously crossing the main street, he went to the telegraph office. At first, he thought it had escaped the worst of the fire. Then, he found only the wall facing the street had survived. The other three walls, along with the roof, had collapsed. He had to step carefully because the lead-acid cells had ruptured, sending the dangerous mixture everywhere.

At the telegraph key, he found the telegrapher slumped forward, thumb resting near the button. The man had died at his job, but had he succeeded in sending out the warning to Miles City and everywhere in between? Slocum wished he knew.

The sound of horses turned him wary. Slocum went to the still-standing wall and peered through what had been a window, but was now only a burned-out square, in time to see a dozen riders vanish down the street, going away from the bank. Caution had been burned into Slocum when dealing with O'Malley and his gang. He waited and was glad for it. Another dozen rode in from the same direction less than five minutes after the first horsemen.

It was as if the entire gang was assembling in the husk of a town.

Using the charred buildings for cover, he slowly followed the riders to a part of town that had escaped the worst of the fires. The structures still stood—and one in particular told Slocum where to find the outlaws. The saloon nearest the bank had burned level to the ground. This saloon had managed to remain untouched.

Slocum considered how many outlaws he could kill if he set fire to the gin mill, then decided not to do so unless he was sure he killed O'Malley in the bargain. Working his way to the back door, Slocum peered in to the littered storeroom. Barrels of beer had already been opened and drained. Cases of whiskey were knocked from shelves, but enough remained to tell him whoever worked as barkeep for the outlaws would be in this room soon.

Watching through the partly opened door, he saw not one but two men come in. Each grabbed a case of whiskey and returned to the saloon. Only then did Slocum go inside. At the door leading behind the bar, he spied on the outlaws singing mournful Irish ballads and dancing jigs on tables, each with a bottle of whiskey in hand.

If they had not all been stone killers, Slocum would have wanted to join their revelry. He watched closely for any sign of O'Malley. The outlaws moved around a lot, blocking a good view of the far side of the saloon.

Slocum sucked in his breath when he heard a familiar lilting voice.

"Buckos, listen up now," called Sean O'Malley. "We done a good job in this town today."

"What's left of it," someone called. The others laughed heartily. O'Malley joined in, took a swig of whiskey, and then set the bottle on the bar. His back was to Slocum. At one time, Slocum might have been squeamish about shooting a man in the back. After seeing what the Schuylkill Butchers did, such qualms were a thing of the past. He would shoot them in the belly or the back and never think twice about it, any more than he would think twice about putting a slug into a mad dog's brain.

"You're so right," O'Malley called. "We burned most of it down, but what's remainin', that's ours! We stole ourselves a fine little town. We've come a long ways from Pennsylvania and fought ever' inch o' the way. Let's toast ourselves!

"To the Molly Maguires!" O'Malley cried.

The chant went up, and died down only when enough of them had to take a deep drink of whiskey to wet their tongues.

"We own this town, lock, stock, and whiskey barrel," O'Malley went on. "We got a steady supply of coal comin' from the hills. This is somethin' that other railroad fella, Hill, wants but doesn't have. His crews cut down the forests, but their engines don't go so far and need more water."

"When we gonna start derailin' those engines, Sean?"

"Soon," O'Malley answered. "When Norris finishes his tracks, then we get into action demolishin' the Northern Pacific tracks. Boys, we're gonna be rich. Norris has political connections to protect us."

"And we got our knives if he don't!"

Slocum stared in cold fury as the assembled men pulled out butcher knives and cleavers and waved them high over their heads. A few began stropping the edges against their aprons and thighs, while others fought mock battles among themselves.

"We're gonna get our own damned country and nobody's gonna stop us!"

Another drunken cheer went up. Slocum realized that O'Malley was crazy enough to think he might succeed. Just because a railroad owner had political connections didn't mean he would use them to protect a wild band of Irish miners. Whatever game Norris played, it stacked the deck against O'Malley and his men. From what the gang leader said, Norris might use them to derail the Northern Pacific, but after getting rid of his competition—or making James Hill's railroad more expensive to maintain—he had no need for cutthroats like O'Malley.

The Irishman might have banged skulls with mine owners in Pennsylvania, but out here he had to fight the entire U.S. Army. They would not take kindly to the men who had slaughtered the soldiers at one of their posts. More than one Indian tribe had discovered that.

Slocum worried that the telegrapher had not sent the warning. He was working on some scheme to find out if the telegrapher had died before he could transmit the message when O'Malley said something that jerked Slocum back to the here and now.

"You men keep an eye peeled on Norris. He's a slimy son of a bitch and will double-cross us when it's in his best interest to do so. But we got a hold over him."

"What's that, Sean?"

"Her name's Etta, and she got auburn hair he's taken a fancy to. All I need to do is get her a knife, and she'll slit the little bastard's throat for us!"

The Schuylkill Butchers laughed at the irony of it. Slocum felt only silent fury. O'Malley had turned Etta over to Norris again as a sex slave, and intended to unleash her fury to kill the railroad magnate when it suited his purpose.

Slocum wanted them all dead and buried in unmarked graves.

15

Slocum slipped out of the saloon and into the cold night. Sweat dried instantly and gave him a chill. He had not even realized until this moment how he had reacted so strongly when he'd heard O'Malley tell his gang about turning Etta over to the railroad owner. The woman was being used as a cat's-paw to remove Norris when it suited the Butchers' purpose.

"That you, Clancy?"

"Yeah," Slocum said, stopping dead in his tracks. He had been so lost in thought about how to rescue Etta that he had grown careless. The Schuylkill Butchers prowled what was left of Sharpesville, and he had not remembered that until being hailed.

"Don't sound like you."

"Drinkin'," Slocum said, coughing. "Lotsa whiskey inside."

"You're not Clancy!"

Slocum lowered his head and charged like a bull. His shoulder drove into the man's midriff and knocked him back two paces. Then they fell heavily, Slocum on top. The man was rattled, but he fought like a wildcat. One punch grazed Slocum's cheek and twisted his face away for an instant. This was all it took for the outlaw to surge upward and throw Slocum to the side.

"Yer one of them local fellers," the outlaw said. "Thought we'd done kilt ya all."

Slocum did not move. He lay on the ground, waiting. His fingers curled around the hilt of his knife, but he did not move to draw it. His patience finally paid off.

"You hurt? Didn't hit ya hard 'nuff to kill ya."

The man moved closer, kicked at Slocum with the toe of his boot, and then stepped back to see what response he got. Slocum rolled with the kick, his knife slipping free as he moved. He lay on his belly.

"Awright, let's git ya into the saloon and—" The man grasped Slocum's collar and heaved.

Slocum was surprised at the man's strength when he picked him up. The outlaw was even more surprised when Slocum drove the knife into his belly. A wet gasp escaped the man's lips as he sagged down. Slocum left the knife in the man's belly as he followed him to his knees.

"Where is she?" Slocum demanded. "The woman O'Malley caught."

"Norris's whore?" The man's eyes went wide. He reached down and touched his wound. Blood leaked out around the blade and turned his fingers red. In the darkness, he might have been bleeding black ink.

The man died without saying another word. Slocum pushed him back, stared down at him, and shook his head. He should have forced the man to tell him what he knew about Etta. It was too late now for that.

Slocum was afraid that Etta was already in Norris's clutches again, but she might be held somewhere around town, waiting for the railroad owner to come for her. Before he went riding off, Slocum had to know for certain.

The festivities continued inside the saloon, so Slocum moved down the street. A few of the Schuylkill Butchers had taken over other buildings, but their celebrations were no less enthusiastic. He considered all the spots where

O'Malley might have Etta a prisoner, and decided on the hotel near the main street. It had escaped the worst of the fire, but scorch marks marred the front wall.

Slocum heard boisterous laughter in the lobby, so he circled the building until he found a back door. It was locked, but only for a moment. It yielded to his knife, leading him into a corridor that led past a dozen rooms to the lobby. He saw three outlaws dancing and whooping it up. One of them banged away at a small piano in such a way that showed he had never played before.

One by one, Slocum tried the doors leading into the rooms. All were empty. A second story required him to get past the men in the lobby. Slocum edged to the doorway and chanced a quick glance. The men were getting drunker by the minute, but he guessed their capacity for booze was far greater than the bottles they had.

Slocum backed up, grasped a doorknob, and tugged hard enough to pull it off. He wound up and threw the knob, sending it out the front door onto the boardwalk. It rattled noisily enough to draw the outlaws' attention.

"What's goin' on?"

"Dunno," said another. The three crowded through the door to see what the ruckus was. Slocum moved quickly, slipping around the corner and going up the stairs to the second story. He had quick looks into the rooms at the head of the stairs before the men came back in, jostling each other and loudly complaining how their drinking spree had been interrupted by a stray dog out in the street.

Slocum worked all the way down the hall without finding Etta. Two of the rooms had been used, but there was no trace of the woman in either. Slocum chewed on his lower lips as he thought hard. O'Malley had not exactly said Etta was already in Norris's hands, but it looked as if this was the case. Hope that he might find her before the railroad owner once more held a leash fastened to her slender throat was gone.

If Etta Kehoe was not in what remained of Sharpesville,

then Norris had her. Slocum went to a window, found a soft-looking spot down in the alley, and dropped out. He had a woman to rescue, and she wasn't here.

Finding the railroad construction had not been difficult. Slocum considered what direction the tracks would come from and headed southeast. From a hill, he looked down onto the camp. In the distance, almost at the horizon, rose a long plume of white smoke as a locomotive steamed away. The workers needed a constant supply of wooden ties and rail. The ties could be cut from the forested areas along the railroad bed, but steel had to be moved from foundries. That meant a constant shuttling of freight from farther east and the end of the line.

Slocum settled down and watched through his field glasses for a spell. The Montana Northern aimed straight for Sharpesville. From there, it would go through the hills directly to the west and on to the coast, completing the line from Minnesota all the way to Washington. Slocum wasn't all that familiar with the territory, but thought that the Northern Pacific had a harder route if James Hill pushed through farther south. Norris would have freight contracts sewed up tight months ahead of the other road.

If he ran his railroad through Sharpesville.

Slocum saw no reason why that wouldn't happen. If anyone in Sharpesville had opposed the railroad—and he doubted that since the iron horse always brought prosperity to the towns it went through—they were long dead. Norris had a willing accomplice in Sean O'Malley. Even as he considered their unholy alliance, Slocum saw a heavily laden wagon rattling in the direction of the construction crew. From the look of the cargo, O'Malley had been actively mining more coal from the hills above Sharpesville. This fuel allowed Norris to run his train until the hoppers were empty, refuel with coal, and then return for more steel rails.

Slocum suspected that J.J. Hill had to burn wood his

crews chopped down. Better to occupy them with cutting timber for railroad ties.

Norris not only worked faster, he worked cheaper, thanks to O'Malley and his gang.

After a long observation, Slocum decided he could learn no more about the railroad camp. He mounted and rode slowly down the gentle incline toward the men driving spikes and laying rail. One looked up, wiped his florid face, and bellowed, "Whatcha needin', stranger? We ain't hirin' nobody's that not Irish."

Slocum tensed at this. He looked around at the number of ginger-haired men. Some leaned on their hammers; others kept hard at work setting spikes and praying that the man with the sledge didn't take off a hand with a careless aim.

"I got a message for Mr. Norris," Slocum said, playing his only trump card. "Supposed to deliver it straight to him and him alone."

"He ain't in camp."

"When'll he be back?"

"Cain't rightly say. He left a couple days ago on the train. Gonna pick up more rail and supplies and be back. Maybe tomorrow."

Slocum tried to figure that out.

"He's not been around for a couple days?"

"Ain't nuthin' wrong with yer hearin', so it must be your brain that's missing a few pieces. That's what I said."

"I need to talk to his woman." Slocum watched the expressions. Nothing but puzzlement.

"Don't know what yer talkin' about, mister."

"His . . . companion. Might be calling her his secretary."

"Ain't nobody like that. Hell, it wouldn't matter if she was as ugly as the ass end of that horse. Jist seein' a woman would be mighty pleasant, and you kin bet none of us'd miss it fer the world."

"We're workin'," piped up another worker, "to git on into Sharpesville. They got whores there. First wimmen we'll have seen in weeks."

"Since that last town," said the man Slocum took to be the foreman. "I swear, never seen wimmen so ugly in all my born days."

If they had seen Etta Kehoe, they would be bragging on it. But if she wasn't in camp and Norris had left two days ago, where was she? Slocum had a sinking feeling that her body might be in Sharpesville's smoldering ruins after all. There had not been any way to look everywhere. If she had escaped the bank, there was no telling where Etta might have tried to take refuge. Any of a dozen devastated buildings might be her tombstone.

"Won't be around for a while? Norris?"

"That's what I heard, but what do I know? I'm only the foreman of this gang of loudmouthed drunks."

"You men always been working on the railroad?"

"Naw, we was miners, but the mine owners got uppity and locked us out."

"Molly Maguires?"

The foreman looked sharply at Slocum. "Proud of it, though bein' in that labor union don't put food on the table no more. Me and the rest of these reprobates moved West, got jobs doin' what we're doin'. Life's hard, but better fer us."

"You and Sean O'Malley," Slocum said. He shifted in the saddle so his hand was closer to his six-shooter if he needed to shoot his way out.

"That's one clever Mick," the foreman said admiringly. "We git our coal from him. Unlike us, he kept on minin'. He's gonna make us all rich."

"How's that?" Slocum asked.

"Mr. Norris, he's promised bonuses if we git to the coast 'fore the Northern Pacific. O'Malley's guaranteein' us that we'll all see an extra hunnerd dollars."

"That much, eh?"

"Every last mother's son of Ireland," the foreman said.

"I'll be back to speak with Norris," Slocum said. He had little interest in the portly railroad owner unless Etta was with him. Then, all he cared about was robbing these hard-working men of their bonuses by ventilating their boss with a few well-placed slugs.

Slocum had spoken to the man's broad back. The foreman had already gotten his crew back to work. The bonus was dangling before them like a carrot in front of a mule.

The twin lines of steel gleamed in the sunlight and ran directly east. It would not be long before trains ran on a regular schedule and connected the Midwest with the West Coast. Slocum pulled away from that, and saw the twin ruts leading back into the hills west of Sharpesville where the coal mines spat out their black load.

If he could not find Etta, he could slow down the progress until she turned up. Somehow, although it was probable, he doubted she was dead. If O'Malley boasted of giving her to Norris so she would kill her sex master, he must have some inkling where she was.

But she was not with Norris, and she certainly was not in the railroad camp.

Slocum's horse kicked up gravel placed down for a solid bed where wooden ties would be laid soon for heavy rails to rest atop them. He followed the twin ruts of the road back into the hills. Soon enough, the railroad builders were out of sight and he was alone in the wilderness. As he rode, he kept an eye out for any of O'Malley's men, but he thought hard on what to do about Etta. He had no expectation of finding her back in the hills.

He heard the mining long before he saw the mine or miners. Slocum drew rein and looked around. A cursory examination showed only the single road leading out of the hills toward the railroad crew. He followed it deeper into the maze of canyons and valleys until he saw the coal mine where he and Etta had spotted the Butchers before.

Counting carefully, he made out eight men toiling at the backbreaking labor of chipping the black rock from the mine, loading it into carts, then moving it to the heavy wagon. Slocum was glad he was patient because two more men came around the mountainside to check the wagon. The others mined. These were the drivers who took the coal down the hill.

Not sure what to do yet, Slocum wended his way up the hillside opposite the mine and put his gelding into the open mouth of the mine there. He settled down behind a big rock, balanced the field glasses on it, and watched. He wanted to know their routine, how the Schuylkill Butchers worked the mine, and if only two men took the coal away.

He also looked for any trace of Etta.

After several hours, he was certain the woman was not in this mine. His hopes for ever seeing her alive again sank, but his desire for vengeance against the brutal outlaws did not fade. A plan formed as he watched the miners break for dinner. It mattered little to them whether it was daylight or not down in the mine, but even burly Pennsylvania miners had to sleep sometime.

By his watch, everyone had turned in sometime after ten o'clock that night. Slocum hitched up his six-shooter and hiked down the hill toward the rude trail cut by the passage of the coal wagon. When he reached it, he paused and remembered the last time he had seen the wagon.

Etta had been chained in the rear of this wagon or one like it when they had rolled into Fort Walker. She had been half-naked and filthy from the coal they had dumped in the wagon. Slocum pushed the memory away, and hunted for what he knew had to be lying around somewhere. In the dark, it took more than twenty minutes for him to find the wood saw used to cut timbers for the mine.

He slipped under the wagon and ran his hand along the rear axle. A rough spot on the otherwise smooth shaft showed where a rock had bounced up from the wheel and nicked the seasoned wood. Slocum began sawing carefully, cutting a notch in the axle. He worked slowly and steadily for almost ten minutes, then stopped and ran his fingers over the notch. How long the axle would last under the load already in the wagon along a rough road was anyone's guess. Slocum hoped it would be several miles before the wood snapped, leaving the driver and his assistant stranded between the mine and railroad camp.

With a full load spilled, they would have to not only replace the axle, but also reload the coal. It was petty, but it would slow down both Norris's and O'Malley's plans. All Slocum could do at the moment was play for time. If he stalled them, he had time to ride to Fort Nealon or some other post and alert the army about what had happened at Fort Walker.

He rolled out from under the wagon and replaced the wood saw where he had found it. Let them think bad luck had struck or, if they saw how the axle had been cut, blame each other for sabotage.

Slocum prowled through the mine and found discarded shirts and other items left by the miners. He tucked these into a bag, along with a few sticks of dynamite from an open case just outside the mine. When he found the blasting caps and fuse, he was ready to ride.

The hike to his horse went quickly. There was a spring in his step because he was fighting back against O'Malley and his cutthroats. They wouldn't run into trouble until the morning when they started rolling for the railroad camp.

The railroad camp would have problems of its own by then.

He reached the camp just before dawn. As with the miners, no guards had been posted. They thought they were working among friends—or at least men who shared the same goals.

Slocum intended to change that in a hurry. He prowled through the camp in search of the supply tent. A solitary coal-oil lamp burned inside it. Putting down his bag, he took out one of the miners' shirts and rolled it up into a thick, smelly rope. He walked to the front of the tent, lit the fuse on a bundle of dynamite, and tossed it into the supply tent.

The man guarding the supplies inside came boiling out. Slocum snared him around the neck with the rolled-up shirt and forced him to the ground until he had choked the consciousness from him. He made certain he did not kill the man. Leaving the shirt, he grabbed his bag and ran. Less than a minute later, the dynamite exploded. For a heartbeat, nothing more happened. Then the coal oil and other flammables in the tent erupted in a secondary explosion that sent sparks flying high into the night sky.

All around him, the railroad crew sprang to their feet. Slocum dropped the items he had taken from the mine in strategic spots, making it appear half a dozen miners had sneaked into camp for the fiery mischief. Satisfied with his salting of clues pointing to the Schuylkill Butchers, he left the camp in turmoil.

The coal delivery would either not arrive or would arrive late in the day. By that time, the railroad foreman would have had plenty of time to fume and fuss and blame the outlaws.

Slocum wished he could see what happened when the two sides came together. The railroad crew might string up the coal wagon drivers. This would set off the miners and be relayed to O'Malley, who might bring his entire gang down.

It would be war. A bloody, dangerous war that would bring the building to a halt.

At least, Slocum hoped it would. He rode straightaway for Sharpesville to search it one last time, just to be sure Etta was not being held prisoner there.

16

Slocum's nose dripped from the smoke still rising from the charred remains of Sharpesville. Only about a quarter of the town remained, and in those buildings the Schuylkill Butchers had taken up residence. Slocum made his way through the burned-out bank, poking through the ashes one last time for any trace of Etta Kehoe. He found one more body, but it was a man. More careful examination made him think it was the dry-goods store owner, Rostropovich.

As he knelt by the body, he heard horses out in the street. Slocum grabbed his rifle and went to the side of the bank where he had blown the hole. He peered out into the dawn and saw a dozen Butchers riding along, muttering among themselves. The best he could tell, they were not pleased with the way their lives were going. O'Malley had promised more than he had delivered so far, and the outlaws wondered when the money from the railroad would begin jingling in their pockets.

Slocum guessed that, after Murphy had been killed, no opposition had remained and O'Malley could do as he pleased. Most of the money the gang stole might have gone into his personal treasure chest. Slocum wondered if he could stir some dissent by stealing O'Malley's loot, but finding it would be almost impossible. O'Malley would protect it—and himself—from the rest of his gang.

The rifle in Slocum's hands provided the best way for him to even the score. Etta was dead, and all Slocum had to keep him in the area was a need for revenge. Using skills he had honed during the war would deliver that. Over the years since Appomattox, his skill as a marksman had not diminished. The only difference now was that O'Malley would be in his sights rather than some Yankee officer.

The knot of riders stopped a dozen yards down the street. Slocum froze and hoped the shadows were deep enough to hide him. Two of the men turned and looked back in his direction.

"Didn't hear nuthin'. Yer jumpin' at shadows."

"O'Malley told us to be sure no one else is alive."

"Hell, that's not what he wanted. He wants that woman. The one he promised Norris."

"Wants her fer hisself," opined another.

Slocum began to worry now. Two had looked back. Now all of them did. He had not made a sound, but something had alerted them. He remained stock-still to keep from drawing further attention to himself.

"I heard somethin' movin'. Over there," one outlaw said, pointing. Slocum was not certain what direction the man indicated since he was hidden by another of the outlaws. "Noisy."

"Might be a dog. Shot one the other day eatin' somebody's arm."

"If you hadn't hacked off all the hands, the animals wouldn't be carryin' 'round the parts."

Slocum seethed. The Butchers had gone through Sharpesville dismembering the dead. This reminded him all over again of the first time he had run afoul of them. The marshal and his posse had been slaughtered, and all he had done was watch. All Slocum had done since was watch. It was time to act.

Slowly lifting his rifle, he estimated his chances of

dropping all six outlaws before they figured out where he was. Chances were not good since the predawn would make his muzzle flash all the more obvious. On his side, none of the men had his six-shooter out. And since they were mounted, it would be even more difficult for them to draw since none wore his gun in a cross-draw holster.

Slocum's finger drew back slowly, but he did not fire when three of the men broke off from the group and rode to the still-intact front of the telegraph office.

"In here. I heard the sounds in here."

"Go take a gander, ya bloody fool," ordered one of the men. Slocum tried to pick out who spoke. This was likely to be the leader. Two of the outlaws dismounted and disappeared into the wrecked telegraph office, only to return a minute later. He saw one shaking his head.

"Rats maybe."

"Damn big rats. Bigger 'n the ones in the mines back in Pennsylvania," protested his partner. "But that wasn't what made the sound. Bricks were knocked over. Something bigger 'n any rat just hightailed it."

"We don't care about anything that's not human," the leader said. "Come on. We got the rest of town to search 'fore reportin' to O'Malley."

"Bugger O'Malley all the way to Dublin. What's he think he is anyway? One of them mine owners back home? I'm tired and don't want to do what he's orderin' us around to do. Let's turn in."

The six men rode away arguing about how diligent they ought to be in their duty. Two of them were hidden by the burned-out ruin of the dry-goods store before Slocum could begin his ambush. He lowered his rifle and took a deep breath that almost caused him to cough.

It was good to know men in the gang weren't happy with O'Malley, but how far that dissatisfaction ran was something he could not tell. With O'Malley dead, would they split up and head in different directions? If so, Slocum could get rid of the entire murdering gang with a single bullet.

Killing Sean O'Malley took on even more importance. Slocum could rid this part of Montana of dangerous, brutal road agents by eliminating their leader.

He bent forward, pressed the brick in the wall into his belly, then tumbled forward and landed in the alley beside the bank. In a crouch, he walked to the street and looked around. The patrol had already disappeared in the direction of the far end of town.

Drifting like a ghost, Slocum started after the men, and reached the junction where burned-out buildings met those still intact. Slocum guessed that O'Malley was either in the bar, though it was almost dawn, or more likely in the hotel asleep. That meant he would be coming out of that building in a few minutes. Craning his neck, Slocum saw a decent spot in a two-story brothel immediately across the street from the hotel.

Going around back, he found a door knocked off its hinges. He went inside, found a flight of stairs, and gingerly tested each step before placing his weight on it. While he wanted to avoid a betraying creak, he was more worried that the rickety stairs would collapse under him.

Reaching the second floor, he went from door to door and peered into each crib. All the tiny rooms, hardly larger than the shakedowns inside, were empty. Some showed signs that the occupants had left in a powerful hurry. Slocum smiled when he saw frilly undergarments still in one room. The soiled dove had probably just pulled on her dress and then run for her life when the fire started.

The fire O'Malley and his murdering thieves had started.

The girls in this whorehouse were probably all dead because of O'Malley. Slocum hoped a few had escaped, although not many others from Sharpesville had reached the dubious sanctuary of the hills. With the Schuylkill Butchers mining up there, anyone fleeing town would have run straight into their guns—their knives.

Slocum completed his reconnaissance of the upper floor, and found a small sitting room at the front where the whores must have sat and dangled themselves out the front window to entice patrons of the saloon to spend their money in a different fashion. He kicked a chair out of the way, moved a table, and laid his rifle on it, then pulled up an ottoman and settled down on it. The lumps in it were uncomfortable, but Slocum doubted he would be here long. He cocked the rifle, moved the table a mite, then sighted in on the front door of the hotel.

O'Malley would exit eventually. When he did, he would get a hunk of lead in his gut.

Slocum dozed for a moment, then snapped alert when he heard something moving in the whorehouse. He laid his rifle down gently, then drew his six-gun and spun about, ready to shoot.

"Don't!" The plea came from the shadows, but Slocum lowered his pistol.

"I thought you were dead," he told Etta. The woman stepped forward. She was filthy. Her once-lustrous hair hung in thick greasy ropes. Her clothing, the clothes that had been so fresh and new from the dry-goods store, were once more in tatters, betraying delicious segments of her bare skin. Her face was so dark from soot that Slocum might have mistaken her for a Negro.

"I thought you were, too," she said. "You never came back!"

"I'm here. It took me a little longer than I expected." Slocum wondered how well his plan to disrupt the coal delivery had gone. He shook that off and stood, cramming his six-shooter back into his holster.

Etta came into his arms and clung to him fiercely. He felt his shirt turning damp from her tears.

"I thought you were dead. I did, John, I truly did!"

"Where were you?"

"Hiding out," she said. "I was with Mr. Parmenter."

"Who the hell's that?"

"The telegrapher," she said, looking up at him. Her eyes still brimmed with tears.

"I saw his body. He was slumped over his telegraph key."

"That must have been someone else," she said. "The two of us found a root cellar and hid in it. Something fell over the door, so they never found us when they went through town killing anyone left." She swallowed hard. "I heard the screams, John. It was awful. I couldn't see what they were doing, but I imagined it from the agony I heard."

"I've got a job to do," Slocum said. "I've got to get back to watching for O'Malley."

"But the telegraph. Did you fix the line?"

"I did. Did your Mr. Parmenter send a warning?"

"There wasn't time. He was certain the line was still dead, then the fires started. They burned us out. We tried to get back to the bank but—"

"Never mind all that," Slocum said, looking over his shoulder at the hotel entrance. He had to kill O'Malley, but something else took precedence. If a message got out, half the soldiers in Montana could swoop down on O'Malley and his cutthroats. Better to have them all killed than just the boss.

"Come on," she said. "Let's get Mr. Parmenter and send the message. If you're sure the telegraph line is repaired, we can do it right now."

Slocum was torn. He could end O'Malley's vile life, if the outlaw leader was even in the hotel, or he could see that a clarion warning was sent along the telegraph route all the way to Miles City. He considered telling Etta to get the telegrapher back to his office, then knew with daylight approaching fast that the Butchers would be moving around the town. Parmenter's specialized knowledge had to be used.

"Please, John. He's across town. It's getting light, and we have to hurry."

"How'd you find me?" He fought against his need to stay and take out O'Malley, but a few more seconds lingering here with Etta could not hurt. The information she had might help him later.

"I chanced to see you skulking about the bank when I went out to find some food. There's nothing in the cellar. Rats had eaten it all before we got there."

"You took quite a chance trailing me," he said. Slocum grabbed his rifle and abandoned the perfect spot to shoot O'Malley. Although he might be able to return and once more get the outlaw in his sights, Slocum doubted it would happen. Such moments were fleeting.

"I had to. I don't think I can get away from town by myself. Mr. Parmenter isn't much help. You saw him. He's not got the skills needed to ride, much less escape from a pack of carrion eaters like the Butchers."

Slocum steered Etta back down the narrow corridor to the stairs. Once outside, he urged her to even more speed. The first light of dawn made them gray blobs, not shadows moving within shadows. With startling speed, the sun came up and lit them brightly, as if they were on stage and had spotlights focused wherever they moved.

"Down," Slocum grated, grabbing her around the waist and bearing her to the ground. They lay beside the boardwalk. Etta struggled a moment, then quieted when she saw two riders making their way up the street, heading in the same direction they were.

"Guards?"

"Cleanup crew," Slocum said. "They're out hunting for survivors to kill."

He longed to rear up, shoot, and take out both men. That would be the utmost folly because he would have the rest of the gang on his neck in an instant. He damned them. He damned Pennsylvania and Ireland and everywhere and anywhere their boots had trod.

"Come on," he said, although the two outlaws were still in sight. He gripped Etta's hand and pulled her along. She was just slow enough that he had to yank hard on her arm to get her into a burned-out shell of a building.

"They saw us," she whispered. "Why'd you—oh!"

She fell silent. Four more outlaws rode along the street

where they had been lying beside the boardwalk. If they had remained where they were, they would have been caught immediately.

"You have to watch and listen both," Slocum said. He was never quite sure what it was that had alerted him to the other men. It might have even been smell, though in the acrid atmosphere of the burned-out town, he had to rely more on sight and hearing. The vibration of the outlaws' horses had come up through the ground. This time.

He looked around to get his bearings. They were in what had been the town bakery. The stench of burned wood here mingled with a more fragrant bread odor. Like a prairie dog, he popped up, looked around, and dropped back.

"What is it, John?"

"We've got big trouble. They're all heading this direction." He knew running was out of the question. "Hide."

"Where?" Etta looked around frantically. She yelped when he scooped her up and carried her to the large bread oven. He yanked open the door, rolled her inside, and followed fast, pulling the door closed after him.

In the dark, cramped space, pressed intimately against the woman, he should have enjoyed it. Instead, his heart threatened to explode in his chest. He heard men poking through the ruins.

"I saw som'thin', I tell you, Barney."

"There ain't nobody here. Look around. See anythin' movin'? Not even the rats are here, and they baked bread. What's that tell you?"

"They baked shitty bread?"

Slocum heard the men laughing and probably playfully punching one another. Only after a respectable time did he push open the oven door and peer out.

"Are they gone?"

"Looks as if they are," he said, but Slocum shut the oven door on a hunch. He was glad because several minutes later two men moved from behind a cabinet, holstered their six-shooters, and went back into the street. They had lain in wait to ambush any unwary survivor.

Slocum pushed the oven door all the way open and helped Etta out.

"That should have been fun, but it wasn't," she said.

"My thoughts, too," he said. Slocum pointed in the direction of the bank, and they set out at a slow walk, watching and listening for the patrolling outlaws. They finally reached the bank and took momentary refuge there.

"Mr. Parmenter's over there. See the tree? The cellar's on the other side, near where the house used to stand."

"Is he armed?"

"Why, I don't know," Etta said, startled. "I never asked. He never showed me a gun or mentioned he had one."

"You'd better fetch him. If I knocked on the door, he might not recognize my voice."

"Be right back," she said, pushing past. She paused, smiled, and then kissed him hard. "For luck." Then Etta dashed to the cellar, rapped several times, and was swallowed up by the ground.

Slocum waited impatiently, but it was worth it seeing Etta emerge from the ground, Parmenter immediately behind her. They hurried to the bank and knelt beside Slocum.

"I thought you were dead, that Miss Etta was only having hallucinations," Parmenter said.

"I saw the telegraph office," Slocum said. "It looks as if the equipment is ruined."

"It's not hard to fix. Even if the telegraph key is broken, I can send by tapping two live wires together. The bug only makes it easier and quicker to send."

"Show me," Slocum said, looking around and then heading directly across the street, angling for the telegraph office. The wall facing the street provided good shelter from prying eyes. He slipped into the wrecked telegraph office, spun, and aimed his rifle out into the street.

"Th-there's a dead man at the key," Parmenter said, stammering.

"Move him, then get to work," Slocum said. "I'll stand watch until you send the message."

"It's like Miss Etta said? You spliced the line?"

"About a mile outside town," Slocum said.

"Very well. I need more battery acid." Parmenter began rummaging about, making a considerable amount of noise, but Slocum was not going to tell him to be quiet.

Etta pressed close and whispered in his ear, "It won't be long now. Then we can be together."

"I hope you're right," Slocum said.

"Got it!"

More crashing and clanking sounded as Parmenter made a new lead-acid battery cell; then Slocum heard the familiar dits and dahs of a telegrapher at work.

"Is it going through?" Etta asked anxiously.

"I don't see why not," Parmenter said. "To be absolutely sure, I need to get a reply. But—"

The roar of a shotgun cut off the rest of his answer.

Slocum ducked, spun past Etta, and fired. His first slug caught the outlaw in the shoulder. He began cocking and firing as fast as he could, as accurately as he could. His fourth slug killed their attacker.

"Run," he said to Etta. "Get back to the cellar and hide. I'll decoy them away."

Slocum kicked through the debris and got into the street. Four Butchers rode toward him. He emptied his rifle at them, winging one. He drew his six-shooter as he ran, getting off one round after another intended more to scatter them than to kill.

He reached the nearby burned-out saloon and whirled around, ready to finish the chore he started. None of the Schuylkill Butchers had come after him.

They had caught Etta and rode off with her dangling between two of them. She kicked and struggled, but was held spread-eagled and could not free herself. Slocum fired at one rider until his six-gun came up empty, hoping to give her a chance to escape. He missed with every shot.

Then he had to figure out a way of escaping the four more who were coming for him. If they caught up with him, he doubted they would just capture him. Instead, he would end up in butchered pieces all over the barroom floor.

17

The floorboards sagged under his weight. Slocum stamped down hard until the partially burned board gave way with a snap. He wasted no time kicking downward again and breaking a second board before jumping down, twisting about, and sliding under the saloon floor. Barely had he ducked down when he heard the thudding of boots entering the saloon.

"Where'd the son of a buck go?"

"Musta gone out the back," said the second outlaw.

"Peter and Kiernan will drop him then."

Slocum waited for the men to notice the broken floorboards, stick their guns down, and blaze away. Instead, they walked past the hole, not even looking down. He looked up through the hole and saw their broad backs. Two quick shots. That's all it would take to end the miserable lives of a pair of O'Malley's killers. Slocum held his fire, though. They had said two more were out back.

He could not take on the entire gang, as much as he wanted to.

Wiggling along in the muck consisting of mud and charred bits of wood and soot, he reached the side of the saloon and peered out from under the floor. Slocum ducked back when he saw a pair of boots come around the back corner.

"I sure as bloody 'ell don't see 'im," complained the man. "He didn't come this way, not 'less he's a bleedin' ghost!"

"We're gonna make him into a ghost. He was real enough back when we nabbed the lass."

"That's the one O'Malley wants, eh?"

"How many beautiful women are there in this town?"

"Alive?"

This set them off into gales of laughter. Slocum dug his toes into the muck, pushed, and squirted out from under the saloon. He got his feet under him and ran for his life. The one Butcher who had come around the saloon had returned to his post behind, sure his quarry would eventually exit the back door. Slocum tried to run lightly, but they either spotted him, or heard his furious dash for freedom.

Bullets kicked up the dirt all around him. He kept running, dodged, and found himself back at the bank. The brick walls gave some protection, but it was four against one. Unless they called more men, he could stand them off for a few minutes while he thought of a way out of his predicament.

O'Malley had Etta by now, probably locking her up in the hotel. Slocum wished now he had resisted Etta's insistence on getting the telegram sent and had taken out the leader of the Butchers. But that was water under the bridge. The outlaws had her prisoner—and they had him boxed in.

He looked back and saw the partly opened door to the bank vault. All the refugees' crazy plans of taking shelter inside the locked vault came back to him. There would be plenty of air in the vault for a single man, but with the outlaws outside, they would have him permanently penned up in a steel-walled coffin.

His toe caught on a box buried in the rubble, and he

stumbled to his knees. He angrily kicked out, then saw the dynamite he had not used before. How it had survived the fire, he didn't know. Heat meant less to dynamite than the sudden jolt given by a blasting cap, but the nitroglycerin that formed the core of a stick was very heat-sensitive. Slocum had warmed frozen sticks of dynamite in hot water when he had worked a mine outside Georgetown, on the opposite side of the Front Range from Denver.

He searched for fuse and blasting caps to no avail. All he had were four sticks of dynamite. He listened to the four outlaws closing in on him and knew he had to work fast. He grabbed one stick, and tossed it in the direction where the bank door had been. He kept the other three, just in case.

"Rush 'im!" an outlaw cried. Three of them tried to crowd through the doorway at the same time. In the instant their gun hands were jammed together, he aimed and fired at the stick of dynamite on the floor in front of them. The explosion was satisfactorily large. It killed one and left the other two in bad shape.

One clutched at his eyes, and the other had lost part of his knee.

Slocum whirled about and fired, more out of instinct than anything else, and winged the fourth man, who was trying to get a shot at him.

Slocum finished him off with a better-aimed shot and then stood. He had three sticks of dynamite and a woman to rescue before O'Malley took it into his head to rape her. For all the outlaw leader's boasting about giving her to Norris so she would eventually kill him, Slocum knew human nature well enough to believe O'Malley coveted her himself.

With his three sticks of dynamite tucked into his belt, Slocum set off for the far side of town where O'Malley made his headquarters. When he came to the junction in the street, the separating line between utter destruction in Sharpesville and the part left standing, Slocum saw that he had his work cut out for him. Dozens of the gang milled around in front of the still-standing saloon and the hotel. The whorehouse he had intended to use for his earlier sniper attack was similarly filled with the Butchers.

What had stirred them up he did not know—and did not want to find out. He slipped around to the rear of the hotel and chanced a quick look in the back door. As fast as he was, one outlaw spotted him and came rushing in his direction.

Slocum opened the door, waited an instant, and then slammed it hard in the man's face. He was rewarded with a loud cry of pain. Slocum whipped open the door again and dispatched the outlaw using his knife.

Heart hammering fiercely, Slocum knelt over the man for a moment, then dragged him into a room and slammed the door behind him. Slocum pawed through the man's pockets and found a few grimy greenbacks in a pocket. He added this to the wad of bills he had taken off other dead outlaws. If he lived to spend the money, he would be in clover for months and months, no matter how profligate he was.

Slocum looked up suddenly when the ceiling creaked. Someone was moving around on the second floor, just above this room. Slocum knew he would never make it to the rear stairs, and going through the lobby was out of the question. If dozens of the Butchers gathered in the street, there might be as many lounging around in the hotel.

A slow smile came to his lips when an idea occurred to him. Slocum used his knife to dig a small circular hole in the ceiling. He jammed the end of a stick of dynamite into the hole so it dangled downward. He stepped back, drew, aimed, and fired. The explosion filled the room with a cloud of plaster and momentarily deafened him, but it also accomplished what he had hoped.

The second-floor room fell down into the room he was in. Tied to a bed was a struggling Etta Kehoe. Two men lay on the far side, one half under the bed. The other had his pants down around his ankles and was trapped in the rubble.

Slocum shot him outright. The other man moaned and struggled feebly. He might have a broken back from the way his upper body twitched and his legs remained motionless.

"John, get me free. Th-they were going to—"

"I know what they were going to do," he said. He used his knife to slash the ropes holding Etta spread-eagled to the bed. "Why'd you let yourself be caught like that?"

"Let myself!" she raged. "I didn't—" She bit off her angry retort, then laughed. "You're joshing me, aren't you?"

"Got to find something funny in all this. Seeing you kicking and fighting between those two owlhoots as they rode away was mighty funny."

"Only if you're remembering it. It was pure hell doing it."

"Come on," Slocum said. He kicked open the door into the hall, and saw men crowding in to investigate what was going on under their noses. He dropped the two sticks of dynamite he had left, pushed Etta out the back door, then fired into the explosives.

The detonation picked him up and threw him past the woman. He recovered, but fiery tongues of orange flame licked outward and forced Slocum to avert his face. He threw up his arm to further protect his face.

"Come on, John. We've got to *go*!"

Slocum didn't need Etta to tell him this. From the hotel, now engulfed in flames, he heard anguished screams of men caught by the unexpected fire.

"Get used to the fire, you sons of bitches. Burn in hell," Slocum snarled. He scrambled to his feet and pushed Etta ahead of him. They had to escape while there was still enough confusion to hide their route away from town.

"Do you have a horse?" she asked.

"We'll have to double up unless we can steal one along the way," Slocum said, veering out of town and heading uphill in the direction of where he had left his gelding.

He hoped that one of the Butchers would ride up so he could donate his horse. None of the outlaws showed any immediate interest in coming after them.

Slocum realized they might not know how the hotel had been set ablaze. Only a couple of the men had seen Slocum, and who would notice Etta was missing?

No one, except Sean O'Malley.

Slocum ran a little faster. Etta was gasping for breath by the time they found his horse. The gelding snorted in disgust, realizing how two riders would weigh him down again. Slocum cinched the saddle tighter, checked the bit and bridle, and then boosted Etta up. Slocum hastily got his foot in the stirrup and pulled himself up.

"Where are we going?" Etta asked.

"Away." He got his horse moving at a steady walk, relishing the feel of Etta's arms around his waist and her cheek pressed into his shoulder. He was stiff and sore, and the wound that had been sewn up earlier itched like ants had burrowed into his flesh, but Slocum couldn't remember feeling better. He had escaped the Schuylkill Butchers. Again.

"Do you think the message got out?" Etta asked after a spell.

"I don't know. Parmenter—that was his name, wasn't it?—I know he sent the message, but if anyone heard it . . ." Slocum's sentence trailed off. The cut in the telegraph line had been fixed. He was sure of that. But what if the outlaws had cut the line somewhere else? Or what if the line had fallen elsewhere on its own? The telegraphs were always out of order because of trouble with the wires and poles, and it seldom had anything to do with men cutting them.

But the telegrapher had seemed cheerful and believed his message had been sent properly. There had not been time for anyone along the line to reply. Slocum kept telling himself that was the case. He and Etta had fought too hard against the Irish cutthroats to let them get away.

"It got through," she said. "I know it. The cavalry is on its way here now. They'd never allow anyone to slaughter all the soldiers at one of their posts," Etta went on with more assurance than Slocum felt. "Fort Walker is an important post, with lots of soldiers."

"If they don't come in force, O'Malley will whup them like he did Major Zinsser and his troopers," Slocum said. He knew how hard it would be for any army commander to believe an entire post could be wiped out and that a single gang of outlaws might number in the hundreds.

"Are we just going to hide out until they come?" Etta asked. Before Slocum could answer, she added, "I'd like to hide out with you until I come."

"What is it you're wanting me to hide?" Slocum asked, grinning.

"I can think of something. So can you. Besides, I'm so tired I am almost falling out of the saddle."

"It's been an ordeal for you," he said.

"All the more reason to make the bad memories go away for a while," Etta said.

Slocum rode along a game trail in the woods and saw a likely-looking spot where he and Etta might linger awhile. He knew they were still close to town, but he had not seen much in the way of tracking skills among the Schuylkill Butchers. His first glimpse of them had been a poor attempt at driving rustled cattle. All they seemed to do well was mine coal and murder.

"We're a few miles away now," Slocum said. "How's—" He never finished his sentence. Etta slipped backward off the horse and landed hard. She smoothed her skirts and went exploring, finding a sunny spot with a lush growth of grass that would be a perfect mattress.

She sat and leaned back on her elbows. Looking up at him on his horse, she smiled and slowly moved her feet back until they were flat on the ground and her knees were bent. She opened them gradually and then pulled at her skirts until she revealed the spot she wanted tended to most.

"Are you coming down to join me?" she asked.

"I'm getting up to do just that," Slocum said, swinging his leg up and over the saddle. He was already uncomfortable. His jeans were too tight in the crotch, and his erection was straining to explode. After making certain the horse was securely tethered, Slocum turned his attention to Etta.

"I can't wait," she said, her bright blue eyes partly closed. She licked her lips slowly, and Slocum thought he would explode then and there.

"You can always start without me," he said, dropping his gun belt and working on his jeans.

"What fun is there in that?" Etta reached down between her legs and stroked slowly through the tangled mat there, then opened her legs a bit more in obvious invitation. By now, Slocum was ready for her.

He dropped to his knees on the soft earth and felt the moist grass crush under his knees. As he moved forward, she grabbed him and tugged insistently. He positioned his hips just right and moved forward another few inches. This time the wetness he felt was warm and inviting and entirely feminine.

"Oh, John," she sobbed. Etta lay back full length on the grass, arms high over her head. He saw how her breasts flattened when she did this. He reached out and brushed open her blouse to expose her fully to his lusting gaze. He dipped low, his tongue flicking like a snake's.

She arched her back and tried to cram as much of her tit into his mouth as she could when he caught the hard little pink nub on the top between his lips. He tongued and suckled and licked. Every time his tongue ran wetly over her turgid nipple, she gasped. She reached down and laced her fingers through his hair, holding him close.

Slocum began to twitch down lower. He remained hidden away in her sheath of female flesh. Whenever he touched her breasts with his tongue, she tensed up all around him, crushing him, trying to milk him. The pressure and heat and wetness worked on him, but he resisted the tide rising in his loins.

He wanted this to last all day. All night!

Working from one succulent mound to the other, he left a wet trail. The gentle breeze blowing through the meadow evaporated the spit and made her moan in even more pleasure.

"I ache, John. My titties *ache*. You make my whole body feel like a raw nerve."

She lifted her legs high on either side of his body and caught her knees with her hands. This collapsed her inner tissues around him even more until he thought it would be impossible to move.

Etta began rocking back and forth, and Slocum knew he could no longer remain still. He matched her movements, in and out, until he found himself in the age-old rhythm of a man loving a woman.

Faster he moved, his hips surging now. He pounded deeper into her, and she took it. She wanted more. She demanded more with her body.

He gave it to her. But the cost was his slowly disappearing control. He felt like he was a young buck with his first woman. She made his body rush, no matter how his mind told him to make it last. The pleasure mounted within until Slocum's hips flew like a shuttlecock. Every inch of his manhood vanished within her, paused, and then slowly retreated. Fast in, slow out.

Etta gasped, lifted her rump off the earth, and ground her hips down into his. This was more than Slocum could endure. He lost all control and began moving hard, fast, wild. His seed exploded from his body like a Fourth of July skyrocket.

As he sagged forward, drenched in sweat and feeling an utter peace descend on him, he took her in his arms. Her legs relaxed, and he lay between them for a moment before rolling onto his side.

"Oh, John," she whispered. "It gets better and better every time we're together like this."

She snuggled close, his arms around her. Slocum stared past, content for the moment, but wondering how long they could linger there. O'Malley and his gang did not have to be good at following a trail. All they needed to do was put a few dozen more riders out to hunt. Even a blind squirrel found an acorn now and then.

But Slocum savored the moment now with Etta. He knew things could change fast. And they wouldn't change for the good if the outlaws found them.

18

"I don't want to stay here by myself," Etta Kehoe said angrily. "You're not running out on me, are you? I thought better of you, John Slocum!"

Slocum held down his irritation. He had heard echoes coming from down the canyon where they rode. The hills were not so steep on either side that they could not clamber to the rim and find their way out of the area, but he preferred to stay in the deep cut through the rocks. The stream running swiftly down the middle provided water for them and his horse, as well as fish for a decent meal. It was easier and quicker tickling a fish or two than it was hunting. Even a single gunshot would alert the Butchers of their quarries' location.

"I need to travel fast. The horse can't gallop more than a few yards with both of us on it."

"I don't want to stay here. This place gives me the jim-jams."

"Better to be a little jittery than to have a slug shot through your pretty head," he told her. Slocum turned his head slightly. Was that the wind? Or a rider approaching?

"Oh, go on. Just don't expect me to be here when you

get back. I'm beginning to think you value your own hide more than you do mine."

"Don't go far," he said, distracted. The sound alerted him now. A rider. He had heard the distinctive click of a shod horse against stone.

She said something more, but Slocum already rode to one side of the canyon, thinking to outflank the rider. He had barely gotten under cover of a stand of trees with low-hanging branches when he spotted the man.

Although he did not recognize him specifically, the man had to belong to O'Malley's gang. There was a look about him, a look more than his red hair or the durable canvas miner's clothing he wore. Slocum slid his six-shooter from its holster and waited for a good shot. If he could get the drop on the man and force him to surrender, he might get important information from him.

Riding farther up the canyon, even with such clear water and abundant fish, might be too dangerous if more of the outlaw gang were there. But if this were the only one of O'Malley's cutthroats in the area, Slocum could ride on fast and hard.

A slow grin came to his lips. As much as he liked the feel of Etta's arms around his waist as they rode, two of them weighed down his gelding to the point of constant exhaustion. With a second horse—the one the Schuylkill Butcher rode—they could make far better time and get the hell out of the area before O'Malley found them.

Just as Slocum was about to call out for the outlaw to throw up his hands and grab a cloud, movement out of the corner of his eye made him freeze. Another rider. Two. Three. The four stopped not ten yards from where Slocum sat astride his horse, worrying that they would turn in his direction and open fire if they spotted him. He had no doubt O'Malley wanted Etta back. Anyone else was destined to be hacked apart.

"No sign of 'em," said the one Slocum had hoped to capture. "Gotta be here somewhere."

"Why?" demanded another. " 'Cuz O'Malley says so? He let them escape from under his nose. He ought to be out here 'stead of back in town livin' the life of Riley."

"What there is of the town," a third said with a laugh. "That cowboy sure blowed the hell out of the hotel. Made O'Malley fumin' mad, it did. He had to go and find hisself a new place to sleep."

"That old lady's boardinghouse is nicer than the hotel," complained the first. "And O'Malley don't have room fer the like of us no more. We kin sleep on the damn ground fer all he cares."

"Don't let him hear you sayin' shit like that," said the one who had remained silent until now. "He's so mad he'll put you *under* the ground."

"That's where we all belong, underground, mining, not traipsin' about lookin' fer a filly and her stud."

"We kin take a break. It's close to midday."

This suggestion won quick approval. The four dismounted and worked to build a fire for their noon meal. Slocum slowly edged his horse away without them hearing. He retraced his path and found Etta sitting on a rock, her chin in cupped hands, looking madder by the minute.

"It's about time you got back," she said.

"Four of them, not a quarter mile ahead," Slocum said. "We've got maybe a half hour before they're on us."

"What?"

"I don't want to get boxed into the canyon. I'd worried about men on our trail. If there are any behind us, they have us sandwiched. The only hope we have is that they haven't figured that out."

"If there are any behind us?" Etta looked shocked. "You never said a word about that!"

"Why bother? There's nothing either of us can do about it. And there's no way we can sneak by the four ahead either. They are camped on the stream. It's wide and rocky there. Wide-open."

"What are we going to do?"

"Climb," Slocum said without hesitation. He looked past Etta to the gentle slope that quickly became steeper as it led to the canyon rim.

"It's a long way, and you said the horse was tired. You're not making sense anymore, John."

"Both of those statements are right," Slocum said, jumping to the ground. "I'll lead the horse to let it rest. We'll start walking. The sooner we do, the sooner we reach the rim."

Slocum did not hear what Etta said under her breath, but it was not fit for polite company. She lifted her dirty, tattered skirts and began hiking. He followed, leading his horse. He had no idea where they would come out, but he hoped it was far away from town. During the past day, they had curved this way and that in the tangle of canyons and valleys until he was confused as to distance if not direction. The sun provided enough guidance for him to know they were moving southward, but he had been wrong about where the outlaws would hunt for them. It was possible he was wrong about more than that.

"Finally," Etta gasped out, pulling herself up to the summit. "We are away from them."

Slocum stopped beside her. From this elevation, he got a good view of the valley where Sharpesville had been built. The smeared black of the burned buildings spread out like some evil patchwork quilt. He took his field glasses and slowly scanned the entire town. When he found a spot where smoke still curled upward, caught on lazy air currents, he knew he had found the hotel he had set ablaze.

Moving on from the burned-out hotel, he stopped when he saw the frantic activity at the nearby saloon. The whorehouse where he had considered sniping at O'Malley bustled with more men than he could shake a stick at.

"What is it?" Etta asked. "You tensed up."

"O'Malley is fortifying what's left of the town. It's not good enough that he has Fort Walker. The railroad is coming through Sharpesville, and he has to keep control."

Slocum saw how the saloon and whorehouse bristled with rifles. It would take a small army to pry the outlaws from those buildings. O'Malley was doing all he could to expand the territory he controlled, and to Slocum's practiced eye, he was doing a damned good job of it. If Fort Walker was secure, Sharpesville would soon be also. The hills where the coal was mined lay completely under the Schuylkill Butchers' command. From there, they could expand along the railroad line, either toward the Pacific or eastward into the Dakotas.

O'Malley might not be as crazy as he'd first seemed. Norris had said the former Molly Maguire wanted to rule his own country. He had a good start.

"What are you going to do?"

Slocum lowered the field glasses and shook his head.

"There's nothing I can do. Going against those buildings now that he has beefed up the walls and turned them into small forts isn't something one man can do. We ride on."

"We could wait for the cavalry," Etta suggested.

"There's nothing to show that Parmenter's telegram was read by anyone along the line," Slocum pointed out.

"It got through. It has to have reached the right people. Otherwise, poor Mr. Parmenter died for nothing."

Slocum didn't bother to tell her that was the way it often happened. Most of the people of Sharpesville had died for no reason, other than O'Malley's lust for power and revenge against wealthy men back in Pennsylvania. No matter what the mine owners had done to O'Malley and his union, there was no call for them to slaughter innocent people the way they had.

The sight and smell of the Schuylkill Butchers hacking up the town marshal still burned like acid in Slocum's brain.

"What would you do if an entire company of soldiers attacked them?" Etta asked.

"Watch," was all Slocum said. He wanted to wash his

hands of this fight. He had plenty of scrip folded and stuffed into his pocket that he had taken from dead outlaws over past few days. It didn't make him rich, but it would keep him in whiskey once he reached a place with a saloon not overrun by killers from Pennsylvania and before that from Ireland.

Etta did not move. She simply stared down into Sharpesville. Finally, she said, "That's my home. I hate to see it in their hands."

"All your people are dead. Your friends, neighbors, everyone is dead."

"Still," she said wistfully, as if there could be some remaining connection. Etta heaved a deep sigh, and her shoulders sagged.

Slocum had turned to mount when he saw movement farther down the hillside in the direction of Sharpesville. He got his foot out of the stirrup and reached for the field glasses he had returned to his saddlebags. He studied the terrain. It might have been wind blowing through branches, but he did not think so.

Then he saw movement again. Coming up the hill. A man's arm showed for a brief instant, then faded into shadow. The skill in moving so silently and with such little exposure worried Slocum. None of the outlaws had shown any such ability, but there could be a few among them who had learned. If this was one, Slocum faced a man who equaled his own skills.

"Here," Slocum said, handing the reins to Etta. "Ride along the ridge for a couple miles, then wait for me."

"What's wrong?"

"Someone's coming this direction. I want you to lure them away."

"What! You're using me as bait?" She was furious that Slocum would consider such a ploy.

"I'll make sure you're all right," he told her. "Hurry. They're moving like the wind." That much was true. If he had not seen the arm with the sleeve flapping on it, he would have believed the bushes' movement was due only to a breeze. However, there was no breeze.

"If I don't show up in a few minutes after you stop, keep riding."

"You mean you'll be dead?"

"Hurry," he told her. He swung her about and got her onto the gelding.

"Don't, John. We can do this together. I can decoy whoever it is here without leaving you."

"No arguments," he said, slapping the horse's rump. The gelding reared, flicked its tail angrily, then trotted off. Slocum wasted no time watching the woman ride away. He ducked down, made for a fallen tree trunk, and flopped behind it. From there he could see the head of the game trail he reckoned the outlaw must be following. There was no other reason the man could move so fast through undergrowth. He had to be following the game trail.

But he wasn't.

The man burst out of thorny undergrowth behind Slocum and swooped down on him before he could swing his Colt Navy around. Strong hands pinned his wrist to the ground, then began to squeeze. Slocum felt the circulation dying in his hand as the six-shooter slipped from his grip.

Rather than fight such superior strength, he suddenly relaxed. The move unbalanced his attacker, allowing Slocum to twist to the side and get his feet up. Lying on his side, he kicked like a mule and forced the man away.

Slocum got to his feet and whipped out his knife. He crouched low, knife extended and ready to face the outlaw.

Only it was not an outlaw he faced. It was an Indian.

The brief hesitation as recognition of his enemy set in was all the opening needed. Slocum was again bowled over and driven to the ground. His knife hand was pinned under one bony knee. The other knee drove mercilessly into his left shoulder. He stared up into sure death. The Indian drew a knife and lifted it to drive down into Slocum's throat.

19

The Indian hesitated, scowled, and looked hard at Slocum.

"You going to stare me to death or use the knife?" Slocum asked.

"Which would you want, Slocum?"

"First, you can get off me. Then you can decide." Slocum grunted when the Indian slipped to one side and lithely rolled to his feet. The knife slid easily into a leather sheath at his belt held by a dull brass U.S. Army buckle. Slocum shook himself to get some of the dust off, then stood. "Been a while." He stuck out his hand. The Indian shook hard.

"You' re getting old. I snuck up on you too easy. Never could have done that before, back in the day."

"Saw you coming while you were still halfway down the hill. I had a woman to get to safety. She did, too."

"Always a story, Slocum," the Indian said. "You can't admit I got you fair and square."

"It'll be a cold day in July when you do anything fair or square," Slocum said, grinning. "You still scouting for the army? You heading up a decent-sized force coming after O'Malley and his gang?"

"O'Malley? That the name? Didn't know."

Both men turned when Etta rode back and drew to a halt a few yards away.

"John, are you all right?" She looked anxiously from Slocum to the scout and back, not certain what was happening.

"Etta Kehoe, meet Sammy Running Bear. We scouted together a year or two back."

"Longer," Running Bear said. "Closer to three. We were down in Ute country. Nasty fellows, those Ute warriors. We were nastier, though."

"Sammy's a Blackfoot. Coming back to the homeland?" Slocum asked.

"I go where the pay is," the Indian said. "We got the telegram and came a'running. True they killed everyone at Fort Walker?"

"Fort Walker *and* Sharpesville," Etta said. "They're thieves and murderers. Nothing's safe from them!"

"Like all white men," Running Bear said in a flat voice. His eyes twinkled when he looked at Slocum.

"Don't ever play poker with him," Slocum said. "He cheats."

"How many men?" Running Bear asked. "My boss needs to know."

"A hundred or so. Maybe not all in town, but split between there, mines up in the hills, and Fort Walker."

"Damn, this is gonna be a war," Running Bear said, shaking his head. "Haven't seen an enemy with so many since we tangled with the Utes down in Colorado. You remember what a pain in the ass that was."

"At least two buildings in town are fortified," Slocum went on. He had no inclination to reminisce. "A saloon and a whorehouse."

"Good choices. Wouldn't mind being holed up in either."

"No whores and they've probably drunk all the whiskey," Slocum said. Running Bear shrugged. "What they do have is plenty of guns and ammo from Fort Walker. The first thing they did after slaughtering all the soldiers was to raid the armory."

"Artillery?"

"Whatever was on the Fort Walker parade ground. Not sure any of them know how to use a field piece, though some of them fired one cannon for the hell of it. I don't think they brought one over to Sharpesville, though." Slocum hesitated, then added, "You never can tell with this bunch. Sly, always coming up with new ideas and ways to kill you."

"Sounds like you admire them."

"I'll kill any of them that moves," Slocum spat out. He saw how Running Bear was goading him, but his anger refused to die. He had seen too much. "I haven't seen any howitzers in Sharpesville."

"That helps. Better get back to Colonel Worthington and report. You think the soft spot to attack is the town?"

"There's no soft spot, but, yeah, Sharpesville is better. And with that much scouting information, the colonel'll think you've actually done your job for a change."

"Only ask those who know," Running Bear said solemnly. "You and your little lady know anything more?"

"I'm not his 'little lady,' " Etta said angrily.

Running Bear ignored her.

"No, I won't," the Indian scout went on, looking straight at Slocum. He flashed a grin, nodded in Etta's direction, then turned and ran back downhill, his footfalls silent. He disappeared in the forest in seconds.

"He's a disagreeable man," Etta said, still miffed. "And what did he mean with that last statement?"

"I was going to send you along with him so you'd be safe with Colonel Worthington's troops, but Running Bear wouldn't escort you." Slocum saw her ire rising even more. "He didn't want to be slowed down." This still did not appease her. "He has to report fast to get the troops into position to attack as quick as possible," Slocum finally said. This did nothing to smooth Etta's ruffled feathers, but at least she wasn't getting madder.

"So we just sit here and watch as the soldiers attack?"

"Something like that," Slocum said. "No reason for us to get on down into the town until afterward, and maybe not even then. There's not going to be a single building left standing by the time this fight is over."

"I hate to see everything down there destroyed," Etta said. "It's my home. Such as it is."

"Such as it was," Slocum corrected. He thought about what she said and had to agree. There was no good reason to stay. Running Bear would report to the cavalry officer, and the attack would be launched when Colonel Worthington decided. If he didn't have enough soldiers, he would be routed. Eventually, there would be a force large enough to handle the Schuylkill Butchers. That might be in a day or a month, but it would happen.

There was no reason for Slocum to stay for the final battle.

"Let's go," he said.

Etta looked at him in surprise. "Go where?"

Slocum had no idea. He had been drifting east. South was as good a direction. Or even back west, although he did not want to tangle with the Driggs brothers again. With Etta alongside him on the trail, Slocum was sure he could avoid the brothers. They would be on the lookout for a solitary cowboy, not one riding with a lovely woman.

"Does it matter, as long as it's not here?"

"There's so much to do," she protested. "I want to see O'Malley kicking at the end of a hangman's rope. And Norris! He has to be stopped, too. Rebuilding Sharpesville is a priority since there must be *some* folks who survived. They'd come back in a flash if there was a railroad running through town. It'd mean prosperity."

Slocum didn't bother pointing out that if Norris was sent to jail or killed, the Montana Northern Railroad would go belly-up and no line through Sharpesville would be completed. He let her ramble on, realizing she had roots in the dead town that were not easily transplanted.

"I could open a—" Etta stopped in midsentence.

Slocum glanced over his shoulder and then went for his six-shooter. He got off a couple shots before his target disappeared.

"Stay here," he ordered.

"John, that was O'Malley! He was spying on us! He knows the soldiers are on the way!"

Slocum already ran hard for the edge of the grove where the leader of the gang had disappeared. When he reached denser forest, he slowed. Etta was right. It had been O'Malley spying on them. Why he was doing such scouting by himself was something Slocum cared not to reflect on. That O'Malley had been listening was good enough.

Movement ahead caused Slocum to lift his pistol and fire twice more. He missed. Plunging ahead, he burst out into a small clearing. With O'Malley were two of his bodyquards. Slocum acted instinctively. One shot to the left, one shot to the right, two men down.

His hammer fell on a spent chamber as he trained his Colt Navy on their leader.

"Yer outta ammo, little man," O'Malley gloated. He kicked each of his guards. Neither stirred. "That's mighty good news fer me. You kin shoot like one of them circus sharpshooters."

"What are you doing up here, O'Malley?"

"We was on our way back from the coal mines when I heard voices. You got more soldiers thinkin' on dyin' in front of my guns?"

Slocum advanced. O'Malley wasn't packing an iron, but he had a long-bladed butcher knife thrust into his belt. When Slocum got within a few yards, O'Malley drew the blade.

"Me and my men, we put in almost a year hackin' up beeves in Chicago 'fore gettin' tired of that. We're miners, not butchers. But we developed a taste for usin' knives on them we don't much like."

"You're cold-blooded killers," Slocum said, reaching down and drawing his knife from the top of his boot.

"That we are, and fer good reason. Those buggered jackasses what owned the mines thought they owned us. Nobody owns Sean O'Malley!"

The Irishman roared and attacked. Slocum stood his ground for only the barest instant. He swung to the side and let the bull's rush go past as he stabbed out with his knife. He felt the tip connect with bone, and then the knife was wrenched from his grip and he was stumbling away.

Slocum looked down. O'Malley had raked his chest with the butcher knife and then dropped it. Slocum's blade was still embedded in the outlaw's wrist.

Not giving O'Malley the chance to pull the knife free from his arm and use it, Slocum duplicated O'Malley's original attack. He cried out loudly and wrapped his arms around the man's bulky body. The two stumbled a few steps and crashed to the ground, knocking the knife free from O'Malley's arm. Slocum used fists and elbows and knees and finally got back to his feet. He faced O'Malley.

"Let's settle this like men. Bare knuckles," O'Malley said. He closed his fingers into bloody fists. The wound on his right arm dripped steadily, but Slocum doubted this was going to hinder the Irishman's attack. And it didn't.

Fists flying, O'Malley came for Slocum. A blow rocked Slocum's head back, and his counterpunch was a feeble tap. He recovered and spat blood. O'Malley had split his lip with his rock-hard fist.

"You canna fight, not with me," O'Malley said. "You're a puny weakling."

Slocum advanced, letting his opponent think he had goaded him into a foolish attack. When he saw O'Malley winding up for a haymaker that would have knocked his head off, he ducked. The blow went past Slocum and left O'Malley's gut open. Slocum pummeled his midriff as hard and fast as he could.

The outlaw grunted, took the punishment, and tried to get closer. Slocum danced away.

"Come and fight, damn yer eyes!"

Slocum saw how O'Malley had slowed. One of Slocum's body punches might have broken a rib. Slocum risked a few blows to his head to get in close and hammer away at O'Malley's right side. When he connected, he knew he had busted a rib in his opponent from the way his fist sank into what ought to be rib cage. O'Malley sagged. He tried to recover, but Slocum was relentless.

Thinking he had O'Malley softened up, Slocum went in for the kill—and almost got killed. Whether O'Malley had been faking or whether he'd summoned a last bit of energy, he swung hard enough to lift Slocum off the ground and throw him onto his back, dazed. Slocum saw O'Malley pick up Slocum's own knife and raise it. Blood hammered hard and loud in Slocum's ears. He had only an instant left to live.

Like an eagle diving from the sky, O'Malley drove the knife downward. Slocum jerked to the side, and the blade sank into the soft dirt. He rolled back and slammed his elbow into O'Malley's head, but the man did not stir. Slocum lifted his arm for a second blow and saw blood on his elbow.

O'Malley had been shot in the back of the head.

Getting to his feet, his knees still shaky and the world doubled all around, Slocum turned to see Etta Kehoe coming toward him. When his eyes focused, he saw she had a rifle in her hand.

"He was going to kill you," she said in a small voice. "I shot him."

"Are accounts square now?" Slocum asked. He took the rifle from her shaking hands.

"Yes," she said, fire coming to her. She spat on O'Malley's body and then kicked at him. "Now I want to do the same to Norris!"

Slocum pried his knife out of O'Malley's death grip and cleaned it before returning it to his boot sheath. He put his arm around Etta's quaking shoulders and guided her from the meadow.

"He'll talk your ears off," Sammy Running Bear said, staring at his commanding officer.

"She doesn't seem to mind," Slocum said. Etta Kehoe pressed close to Colonel Worthington. He had no idea what they discussed, but it probably had something to do with the assault that had taken several days against the Schuylkill Butchers in Sharpesville. The colonel had sent for reinforcements to pry them out of Fort Walker, but with O'Malley dead, the fight might not have been as fierce as the officer bragged on.

"You going to take your woman back?" Running Bear stared hard at Slocum.

"Not my squaw," Slocum said. "Is the colonel married?"

"No."

"Might be his then," Slocum said. He had no intention of remaining here to rebuild the town, but from the hints he had from Running Bear and some of the soldiers, Worthington was considering moving his command to Fort Walker—and it was not simply to fill the void left by Major Zinsser's death. Slocum saw how the colonel looked at Etta and how she looked at him.

"You are getting old. You give up too easy."

"What makes you think I have a dog in this fight?"

Running Bear considered this, then said, "You should. She'd make you a fine squaw."

Slocum laughed. He had a rested, fed horse, a pocketful of greenbacks taken from dead outlaws, and horizons in all directions. He shook hands with Running Bear, then mounted. There was no need to say good-bye to Etta. She wouldn't care, and if she did, she would get over her loss in a while.

Slocum was as sure of that as he was that he could put fifteen miles behind him by the time the sun set.

Watch for

SLOCUM AND LITTLE BRITCHES

355th novel in the exciting SLOCUM series
from Jove

Coming in September!